THE GOLDEN CHRISTMAS

THE

GOLDEN CHRISTMAS

A Tale of Lowcountry Life

WILLIAM GILMORE SIMMS

Introduction by David Aiken

UNIVERSITY OF SOUTH CAROLINA PRESS

Introduction © 2005 David Aiken

Cloth edition published as *The Golden Christmas: A Chronicle of St. John's, Berkeley, Compiled from the Notes of a Briefless Barrister* by Walker, Richards and Co., 1852
This paperback edition published in Columbia, South Carolina,
by the University of South Carolina Press

Manufactured in the United States of America

15 14 13 12 11 10 09 08 07 06   6 5 4 3 2

Library of Congress Cataloging-in-Publication Data

Simms, William Gilmore, 1806–1870.
   The golden Christmas : a tale of Lowcountry life / William Gilmore Simms ; introduction by
David Aiken.
      p. cm.
   ISBN 1-57003-612-8 (pbk. : alk. paper)
   1. South Carolina—Fiction. I. Title.

   PS2848.G6 2005
   813'.3—dc22

                                                                            2005050366

ISBN 13: 978-1-57003-612-5

INTRODUCTION

The Golden Christmas is a plantation romance written by William Gilmore Simms (1806–1870), the father of Southern literature, and presented as a gift to his native city. Serialized in January and February of 1852 before being released in book form as a chronicle of the social customs of people in Berkeley County, South Carolina, the story highlights Christmas celebrations and social habits of antebellum Charlestonians. This edition of *The Golden Christmas* is a photo-offset reproduction of the only edition Simms saw through the press. It has been enlarged 25% to make it more readable. Knowledge obtained from this plantation romance is invaluable to a better understanding of the Christmas decorations and celebrations, as well as the manners and dress of antebellum Lowcountry Carolinians. The book is also entertaining, because by 1852 William Gilmore Simms was a master story teller, writing carefully about his own world, a world he both understood and loved. By alluding to Shakespeare's *Romeo and Juliet* and Charles Dickens's *A Christmas Carol*, Simms increases the reader's interest in the loves and adventures of two young bachelors looking for wives.

The spirits of Romeo and Juliet receive a Southern twist in an 1851 romance set in the Charleston area. Ned Bulmer is in love with Paula Bonneau. The English Bulmers and the French Bonneaus have been feuding for one hundred years when the star-crossed lovers begin the frustrating task of obtaining the blessings of elders as yet unaware the two are determined to wed. Ned enlists the aid of best friend Dick Cooper, the story's narrator, who is himself in love with Beatrice Mazyck. The two young men begin a merry chase in pursuit of their true loves during the holiday social season, a chase which will reach its peak at the Bulmer plantation where friends and relatives are gathered to celebrate the one-hundredth-year anniversary of the family's first Christmas at the Barony. It just so happens that the Bulmer plantation is situated in the same parish where the Bonneaus and the Mazycks also maintain family plantations. Matters become more complicated when Dick discovers that Ned Bulmer's father and Beatrice Mazyck's mother are secretly planning an "arranged marriage" for Ned and Beatrice.

The Golden Christmas was from start to finish a thoroughly Charleston creation. It had a native Charleston author working with a Charleston publishing company using Charleston printers engaged in the business of operating a steam-powered press. It portrayed Charleston's long standing relationship with the Lowcountry plantations then so firmly connected to the city. It also gave life, voice and history to a diversified population of town and country dwellers. The manners and morals, fashions and furnishings, architectural accomplishments and agricultural advancements of the Lowcountry's people were all portrayed in a story depicting the social and psychological changes at work within the community.

Because it was written for and about the very people William Gilmore Simms routinely passed on the streets of Charleston, *The Golden Christmas* today provides one of the most comprehensive and accurate chronicles of the lifestyles of antebellum Carolinians. The format Simms used to tell his story was that of the historical romance, a nineteenth-century variation on the epic poem which travelling storytellers carried from village to village in some of the world's most ancient literature. The historical romance was uniquely suited for writers attempting to produce a national literature. Simms, like his contemporaries James Fenimore Cooper and Nathaniel Hawthorne, had already achieved popular success by writing historical romances. But unlike them, Simms was helping to create a sub-genre, the plantation romance, when he wrote *The Golden Christmas*.

The idea of using Christmas festivities in a plantation romance was employed by Simms several years before he wrote *The Golden Christmas*. His novelette, *Maize in Milk: A Southern Story of Christmas*, was published serially in 1847 in *Godey's Lady's Book*. Louis Godey, impressed by the continued success of Charles Dickens's *A Christmas Carol* (1843), apparently felt that Simms might further benefit by turning *Maize in Milk* into a Christmas book "a la Dickens." It was suggested that Simms add enough to the story to make it suitable as a separate publication. Simms considered the suggestion, discussed it with the publishers Carey and Hart of Philadelphia, but he never did present *Maize in Milk* as a separate publication. By the time Simms did write a Christmas story "a la Dickens," he was in an impish frame of mind: if American publishers were going to insist upon looking to England for story ideas, he would take the best of England, turn it upside down, and give it a Lowcountry twist, using the charm and flavor of Charleston spiked with an ample dose of comedy. The result was a Christmas story "a la Dickens," with a double helping of Shakespeare, a dash of Jane Austen, and enough Simmsian humor to suit the taste of almost anyone living in South Carolina.

Although Simms enjoyed a literary challenge as much as he appreciated a good joke, he was truly dedicated to pleasing everyone for whom he wrote. Once he had committed himself to writing for Lowcountry Carolinians, he faced a real challenge. He needed a basic plot which would appeal to young people even as it conjured up warm memories and emotions in their elders. He also needed to fill the story with scenes and characters interesting enough to delight all of his readers. Comedy would become the glue to hold everything together. But a shared sense of history had to be evoked in order to make the story work as the vehicle of reconciliation Simms intended the novel to become.

As a student of the Bible and a firm believer in Divine Providence, Simms held Christmas in high regard. The love people displayed for one another during the Christmas season was a reflection of God's love for man. God's loving man was reason enough for joyful Christmas celebrations. This conviction led Simms to celebrate Christmas by writing newspaper articles on the history of Christmas, poems in which Christmas celebrations were the focus, and the earlier plantation romance, *Maize-in-Milk*, which had begun with one Christmas celebration and had ended with another. *The Golden Christmas* is very different from *Maize-in-Milk*. For one thing, it showcases the addition of a Christmas symbol so commonplace now that few readers today could imagine Christmas without it.

Maize-in-Milk does not have a Christmas tree. But the tree in *The*

Golden Christmas is "a beautiful cedar, carefully selected, and brought in from the woods, the roots well fitted into the half of a huge barrel, rammed with moss, the base being so draped with green cloth as to conceal the rudeness of the fixture." Tiny glass lamps of different colors are lighted among the branches from which a variety of gift-wrapped packages are hanging.

Why no tree in *Maize-in-Milk*? Simms was presenting in 1847 an "authentic" Southern Christmas. Elaborate as they were, decorations for plantation Christmases did not then include Christmas trees. A letter Simms wrote in December 1850 to his friend James Lawson in New York provides a clue to the appearance of a tree in *The Golden Christmas*: "My wife is eagerly looking for the arrival of Jenny Lind in Charleston when she proposes to visit the City Hotel for the purpose of hearing the Swedish Nightingale." On 23 December 1850, Charleston's *News and Courier* contained information about the renowned singer's Charleston visit: "Last evening, at her lodgings, a Forest tree was placed at her window, decorated with variegated lamps, which attracted much attention." About the same time, the influential *Godey's Lady's Book*, published in Philadelphia, reproduced an etching of Queen Victoria's Royal Family gathered around their Christmas tree in Windsor Castle. The etching, originally printed in England in 1848, had catapulted the Christmas tree into the world of London fashions. By 1851, Charleston had adopted one more European symbol for celebrating Christmas. The tree in *The Golden Christmas* demonstrated the progressive nature of Charleston, as well as the continued influence Europe had on the Lowcountry. It also underscored Simms's commitment to authenticity.

Simms drew on personal experience to a greater degree than might be expected. When not secluded to write, he lived an extroverted life. He was much in demand for parties, enjoyed attending theatrical performances and frequently opened his plantation home Woodlands to guests. In August of 1850, Simms and a number of Charleston's most prominent men served as senior managers for a ball held at the Moultrie House on Sullivan's Island. The event received extensive coverage in *The Charleston Courier*: the senior managers "appeared in citizens' dress, wearing rosettes upon their left breasts and attending ladies in costume." Simms later used this ball as a setting for *Flirtation at the*

Moultrie House: In a Series of Letters from Miss Georgiana Appleby to Her Friends in Georgia, Showing the Doings at the Moultrie House, and the Events Which Took Place at the Grand Costume Ball, on the 29th August, 1850; with Other Letters, which was printed by Edward C. Councell in Charleston before year's end.

In *The Homes of the New World; Impressions of America*, the Swedish novelist Fredrika Bremer tells of a party given on 2 June 1850 by Mrs. William Howland where Simms was a guest. Her description of the event includes many of the same party elements found in *The Golden Christmas*. After describing the party as "beautiful" and "very charming," the novelist reports, "Mrs. Hammarskold (Emilie Holmberg) sang very sweetly; I played Swedish dances; people talked, and walked about, and drank—*tout comme chez nous*. I saw Mr. Simms, one of the best poets and novelists of South Carolina, this evening. He is an enthusiast for the beautiful scenery of the South, and that pleased me, and therein we agreed very well."

Simms's dialogue in *The Golden Christmas* is another example of his commitment to authenticity. Once deemed "proper" English, the mother tongue brought to Charleston in her colonial period by representatives of the Crown had changed considerably through the years. The port city attracted so many visitors and new settlers, speaking languages other than English, that she soon found her King's English being added to and revised. Charleston children quickly acquired new pronunciations of English words as well as smatterings of those non-English languages they found appealing to the ear and tongue. They were especially susceptible to Gullah spoken by members of the city's black population. It was expressive, satisfying, spontaneous and fun. Even parents insisting upon purity of language occasionally spoke Gullah themselves. Over time the very spelling of some English words began to change. What Charleston lost in purity of language, though, was more than compensated for by the rich and abundant vocabulary her population acquired. Today's readers of *The Golden Christmas* may well need a dictionary to appreciate fully this treasure chest of marvelously expressive words. Many of the puns in this story, which is filled with them, make sense only in light of the meaning Charlestonians gave to what were then commonly used words. The word *bark*, for instance, was used in connection with the sound a dog makes, a particular kind of sailing ship, a dye or tan using bark, rubbing skin off, a medical treatment, and a medicine derived from trees or woody plants.

Charleston in the 1850s was, of course, rich in more than language. Wardrobes for both men and women were colorful and ornate. Dick Cooper's cravat, the scarf worn like a tie about his neck, is probably made of soft silk since Ned Bulmer is able to form it into "a perfect rose under Dick's chin," by gathering the material into folds to resemble a rose. The Valenciennes tippet worn by Madame Girardin is a long scarf-like accessory made of exquisitely floral-patterned lace from Valenciennes, France, a city noted for its lace as early as the fifteenth century—a time when lace was so valuable that the theft of one small piece could land the thief in jail for a prolonged period. Furthermore, the tippet required considerable material since it was draped around the neck and over the shoulders, falling far below the waistline.

In the London which Charles Dickens depicts in *A Christmas Carol* (1843), this one article of clothing would be worth more money than Bob Cratchit could earn in a year. For all its industry and mercantile activity, Londoners were generally less well off than Charlestonians. The working class in London had less access to clothing, food, shelter and medical care than Charleston's slave population. In Carolina, public opinion and state laws came down hard on the slaveholders who neglected or mistreated members of their work force. Nothing in Dickens's London protected the working class from cradle to grave. As Dr. Samuel Henry Dickson (1798–1872)—a native Charleston physician—stated in an 1859 lecture he gave in Philadelphia on pain and death, people born into poverty in large and flourishing cities often lived miserable lives:

> Being poor, the atmosphere he breathes is poisonous; the food he eats is garbage; the water with which he quenches his thirst is saturated with abominations; his clothing is rags; he earns his foul morsel through vice and humiliation; throughout the whole of his existence of sorrow and discomfort—this living death—he is watched by those who live around him in ease and comfort, and enjoyment, as dangerous to them, both morally and physically; and if he does not fall into the hands of an executioner, may consider himself fortunate to be permitted to expire in the ward of some hospital.

The lives of Carolina slaves were different. As Simms makes clear in *The Golden Christmas*, slaves had property over and above what was provided by the master. Many had their own gardens and livestock as well as the means to earn money for themselves and still have enough time to spare for pleasant pastimes.

In some respects, then, *The Golden Christmas* can be viewed as a Southern Christmas Carol. It is possibly a response to *Uncle Tom's Cabin* as well. Although Harriet Beecher Stowe's book was published on 20 March 1852, after *The Golden Christmas* was already in book form, her story had also been first serialized. Whereas Stowe's *Uncle Tom's Cabin* began to appear in the *National Era* in 1851 and continued to appear serially into 1852, Simms's *The Golden Christmas* was not read until 10 January 1852 when the first part appeared in the *Southern Literary Gazette*. The second part was published 24 January and was followed by the concluding portion 10 February 1852. Simms was an avid reader and a literary critic, routinely writing reviews of works by other authors. It is therefore likely that Simms had already seen installments of *Uncle Tom's Cabin* before he completed *The Golden Christmas* in serial form even though his book was published in February, a month before Stowe's.

Short as it is, *The Golden Christmas* contains a little something for everyone. For male readers, it includes deer hunting, wild boar hunting and jousting. It treats female readers to a love story replete with descriptions of fashions, food, and home interiors. Pun-lovers, lovers of comedy, and lovers of history get their fill. There is plenty to satisfy the curiosity of the younger generation as well.

Simms's Charleston was like a city university. Young people were home trained at an early age and, already able to read, could enter one of Charleston's many schools after being exposed to an array of cultural opportunities. Simms himself had begun to write poems when he was eight. By the age of twenty-one he was married, had passed the bar, and was settling into a legal practice when his first child was born the next year. Along the way he had written for newspapers and had published one volume of poetry which was closely followed by a second.

A number of Charleston's citizens had extensive personal libraries and loaned out books to neighbors on request. The city's first subscription library had opened in 1748, a hundred years earlier. By 1850 the free black community in Charleston had several libraries of its own. As Bernard E. Powers Jr. points out in *Black Charlestonians: A Social History, 1822–1885*, only one percent of the adults in Charleston's free black community of 3,441 people was not able to read or write in 1850. This high literacy rate was due largely to the efforts of men like Thomas Bonneau.

A free-black man with a keen interest in both contemporary and classical literature, Thomas S. Bonneau was a prominent Charleston teacher with ample income. He was also a slaveholder and the owner of an extensive plantation outside the city. In 1803 he became a founding member of the Minor's Moralist Society formed in order "to educate orphan or indigent colored children," and in 1807 he established a school to educate the children of the Brown Fellowship Society. The Bonneau Literary Society and Thomas S. Bonneau's school had a significant impact on free blacks who built on what Bonneau had begun. Later free-black schools would hire both black and white teachers. When the Swedish writer, Fredrika Bremer, visited Charleston's free-black schools early in the decade of the 1850s, she was impressed by the breadth of study they offered and noted that one school had texts exactly the same as those used by white children.

Simms's Romeo and Juliet motif had relevance for both blacks and whites living in the city of Charleston. Divisions within the white community were mirrored within the black community where members of the Brown Fellowship Society, composed of prosperous and cultured mulattoes, kept their distance from the Society of Free Dark Men whose members viewed with disdain what they deemed the pretensions of the mulatto elite. As Powers notes, the latter group mingled with slaves in grog shops, at nocturnal balls, at the race track, at church and in a variety of amusements. The brown elite, many of whom were slaveholders, avoided social contact with slaves. Arranged marriages were not uncommon in this group where "only families of similar socioeconomic backgrounds intermarried." In 1868, one former slaveholder, a free black descended from a Santa Domingo French family, violently opposed the marriage of his daughter, Frances Rollin, to William Whipper. The Rollin family members, with the exception of Frances, considered themselves French and saw the Whipper Family as "small people" and "negroes" unworthy of their notice.

Pride and prejudice were surely keeping more than one house divided against another in Charleston when in 1852 Simms offered his adaptation of the Romeo and Juliet theme of star-crossed lovers intent upon a union their elders opposed. A black Romeo and a brown Juliet could relate as easily to Simms's story as could a tall English Romeo and a petite French Huguenot Juliet.

Maintaining his focus on pride and prejudice while departing from the Romeo and Juliet motif, Simms ends *The Golden Christmas* with a humorous sketch centered upon the theft of a pig, which is actually a story in its own right. Zacharias, the gentlemanly body servant of Major Bulmer, complains that Jehu, the city-bred carriage driver for Miss Janet Bulmer, has stolen, slaughtered and eaten one of Zack's fattest pigs. Zach does not rank Jehu among his acquaintances, thinks his manners are vulgar, and judges his language low and unseemly. Jehu eyes Zach the same way "a wild western hunter would eye a Broadway dandy." A mock trial ensues. The master's final judgment finds Jehu "guilty, and sentenced to the loss of three of his lean pigs to Zacharias, in compensation for his fat one." Major Bulmer adds, however, "If you keep honest till next New Year's, Jehu, and kill no more fat pigs of other people, I will give you three out of my stock." The decision doesn't satisfy either Zack or Jehu. Zack is certain Jehu will continue to steal his pigs. And Jehu continues to feel he should not be blamed for stealing fat pigs because it is in his nature to steal them, even though he would never steal anything else.

Simms's knowledge of the way human nature remains at war with the expectations of society is tucked neatly into this comic conclusion. Romeos will continue to "steal" Juliets from their families. Writers will continue to slaughter their longer works and to disguise the stolen portions in shorter works designed to keep bacon on the table, just as Dickens had adapted a Christmas-goblin story from a chapter in his popular novel *The Pickwick Papers* in order to suit his needs in creating *A Christmas Carol*. Likewise, American authors will continue to "steal" material from England's literary masters and adapt it to suit the tastes of their own readers.

Just as *Uncle Tom's Cabin* was written to appeal to readers of the *National Era*—an abolitionist publication—*The Golden Christmas* was written for a Charleston audience. Out-of-towners could not fully appreciate the settings Simms employed. Someone not familiar with Charleston, for instance, would find Dick Cooper's shopping expedition at Kerrison's with Madame Girardin only mildly amusing, that of a bachelor stuck assisting a picky old lady in her selection of purchases. An antebellum Charlestonian, though, would have seen Kerrison's as it was described by Rosalie Roos, the Swedish author who depicted Kerrison's full splendor in *Travels in America: 1851-1855*. According to Roos, Kerrison's was 270 feet long and contained "millions of dollars worth of goods." Located at the corner of King and Hasell streets, it was "said to be the world's first department store." Four large glass doors opened on the enormous space. Cast iron chandeliers with milk glass globes for gas light hung from a carved ceiling supported by ornamental columns. Long aisles of mahogany counters on either side ran to the back of this huge room, where a few steps led up to a small alcove draped with silk curtains and brilliantly colored rugs. One semicircular counter with glass drawers displayed all kinds of gloves. Behind a railing, book keepers enjoyed the cheerful fire of their stove. Free-standing iron stoves scattered about warmed the rest of the store. Round cast-iron stools fixed to the floor and covered in dark red velvet ran the length of the counters. The goods kept in shelves and drawers on the main floor were "scrupulously separated into department after department" and consisted of "most anything anyone could desire."

Simms's Charleston readers did not need the descriptions of Roos to know how far out of his element Dick Cooper was swimming when he went shopping with Madame Girardin. They had seen this feminine paradise; they knew just how long a lady could linger in such a setting, and about how long a young bachelor could bear the tedium of making selections in which he was not interested.

Today's readers and yesterday's out-of-towners might be tempted to think of Russell's Bookstore as primarily centered on the sale of fine books. Simms needed only to hint about the store's art collection in *The Golden Christmas*, because Charlestonians would have known John Russell's passion for fine art which he made available to his neighbors.

His support of fine art and praise-worthy artists was legendary in the city. Here again Simms employs setting to establish an "insider's joke." Russell's Bookstore is the one place Dick Cooper would have been likely to linger, if Madame Girardin's contempt for some of the modern art had not brought a halt to the day's shopping excursions.

To satisfy the expectations of his Charleston readers, Simms touches on the familiar associations they have with Christmas: fireworks, candles nestled in holly on mantles, games of whist and backgammon, a Yule log and a visit from Father Chrystmasse. Singing, dancing, horseback riding, promenading, and play acting are also included in *The Golden Christmas*. Making eggnog is depicted as the Southern social event it really was in the 1850s. Young ladies giggle as beau after beau takes his turn beating egg whites until his arms give out.

In *A Plantation Christmas* (1934), the Upcountry South Carolina author Julia Peterkin declares: "Christmas is no holiday gotten up for children, but a season which is enjoyed by the grown people with the utmost enthusiasm." Peterkin was echoing a sentiment Simms's generation embraced in the South where Christmas had long been linked to the spirit of amour and the pursuit of true love at the height of the social season. South Carolina was one of the colonies where Christmas celebrations had not been smuggled in by a Dutch Saint Nicholas bearing gifts for children. As Simms knew full well, America's divided loyalties to Christmas traditions actually started in Europe where Saint Nicholas had been banished from most of its countries after the Protestant Reformation. In England Saint Nicholas had been replaced by Father Chrystmasse, a fictive sponsor of adult fetes concerned with amour. Druid in appearance, the good saint was closely connected to nature, lush evergreens, and nature's bountiful harvest. Kissing under the mistletoe, which grew in abundance in the South, was a custom dating back to Ole England. It was a custom many New Englanders would have found scandalous in 1850. The Dutch who introduced Saint Nicholas to puritan New England brought a child-loving, gift-giving saint with them to a region where Christmas was observed passively, not actively as in the South.

Simms conveys the message that Father Chrystmasse came to America first, by having his characters celebrate Christmas in the Lowcountry as their ancestors had celebrated it there one hundred years earlier. During the same hundred years, New England people had often suffered greatly for any display of Christmas cheer. At one point the making of mincemeat pies had been forbidden in Boston, because of its association with Christmas celebrations. There had been fines to pay if a Bostonian was caught decorating a home with greenery. When Christmas fell on a weekday, Bostonians could be jailed for playing ball on the street instead of going about work as usual. Like Scrooge in Dickens's *A Christmas Carol*, many a New Englander had long considered the idea of taking off a day from work to celebrate the birth of Christ as nothing short of frivolous. Oddly enough, Christmas celebrations did not truly find favor in New England until Sunday school teachers proposed the idea of enticing more children to attend church with offers of gifts at Christmas.

Simms concludes his account of the visit of Father Chrystmasse to the Bulmer Barony with these words: "But who played the venerable Father, and who played the sweet voices! What matter? Better that the juveniles should suppose that there is an unfamiliar Being, always walking beside them, in whose hands are fairy gifts and favours, as well as birch and bitterness!" By placing Father Chrystmasse in the plantation home, Simms expands the importance of good behavior beyond the church. Hospitality is not the only virtue that begins at home. So, too, does the belief in Divine Providence as an ever present witness to every act, good or bad, no matter where it occurs. In Simms's South, well-mannered behavior was not saved for Sunday, nor was it set aside for special events. It was to be practiced everyday, all year round, as much in the home and community as in the church. The goal for young men, for example, was the widely hailed ideal of the Southern gentleman. The expected result was an ideal of antebellum Southern character, as outlined in *The Southern Field and Fireside* (19 May 1860):

A gentleman is not merely a person acquainted with certain forms of conventionalities of life, easy and self-possessed in society, able to speak, and act, and move in the world without awkwardness, and free from habits which are vulgar and in bad taste. A gentleman is something beyond this. At the base of all his ease and refinement, and tact and power of pleasing, is the same spirit which lies at the root of every Christian virtue. It is the thoughtful desire of doing in every instance to others as he would that others should do unto him—*He* is constantly thinking, not indeed how he may give pleasure to others for the mere sense of pleasing, but how he can show them respect, how he may avoid hurting their feelings. When he is in society he scrupulously ascertains the position of every one with whom he is brought into contact, that he may give to each his due honor. *He* studies how he may avoid touching upon any subject which may call up a disagreeable or offensive association. A gentleman never alludes to, never appears conscious of any personal defect, bodily deformity, inferiority of talent, or rank, of reputation, in the persons in whose society he is placed. He never assumes any superiority—never ridicules, never boasts, never makes a display of his own powers, or rank, or advantages; never indulges in habits which may be offensive to others.

Charleston readers knew William Gilmore Simms as surely as they knew Kerrison's many splendors and John Russell's passion for art. Simms had been one of their attorneys, a state representative, a frequent public speaker, and the editor of city and state newspapers and magazines. His fondness for claiming he had once been tempted to become a preacher was widely known. It is interesting to note, therefore, how little preaching Simms does in *The Golden Christmas*. A student of the Bible will spot his biblical allusions which, though plentiful, are well integrated. Simms does allow Major Bulmer to talk about driving out the "evil spirits" of prejudice and hatred with love, and to speak of "this blessed season, when all the influences of life are meant to be auspicious to human happiness." Remaining true to his commitment to religious freedom of worship, though, Simms does not impose his own convictions on his readers. The spiritual message, consistent with the Christmas setting, can be read throughout the novel from the first chapter to the last, but readers not interested in its spiritual dimensions can read the novel purely for entertainment. This harmony between enlightenment and entertainment made Simms's plantation romance a choice gift for Charleston readers of any religious persuasion.

Today's reader of *The Golden Christmas* without easy access to antebellum newspapers, magazines and books may find it difficult to envision the period in America's history during which Simms was writing. Few readers are aware of the restrictions New England societies once placed on Christmas celebrations, or the way New England authors like Oliver

Wendell Holmes and Hezekiah Butterworth lamented their region's somberness and absence of celebration. Fewer readers still are acquainted with the once widespread problem of pig theft. While pigs often ran wild on plantations in Carolina, they ran the city streets of New York well into the 1860s, tempting the poor and the hungry. Fashionable New Yorkers were equally troubled by the dust and mud the loose herds of pigs kicked up and onto their clothing. Complaints from disgruntled pedestrians found their way into the news on a fairly regular basis. As a frequent visitor to the North, especially to New York City, Simms was well aware of the issues and problems debated in Northern newspapers.

Pig owners in the Lowcountry, whether slave or master, did not have to wait months for justice rendered by an exhausted judge whose verdict was sure to be protested in local papers, as often happened in New York City. The Lowcountry folk who could settle their own pig-theft problems without legal intervention were likewise free to celebrate Christmas with muskets and cannon and fireworks, whereas New Yorkers were forbidden by law to so celebrate. Christmas did not even become a "legal" holiday in Massachusetts until 1856. The Massachusetts author Oliver Wendell Holmes described the Boston of his youth as "a Boston with no statues, few pictures, little music outside the churches, and no Christmas."

Although Charleston does not escape Simms's gentle social satire in which he humorously chides his city for flaws in her makeup, *The Golden Christmas* focuses more on the many freedoms Charlestonians enjoyed rather than on the sometimes thoughtless ways they behaved in both their public and private lives. Since Christmas is a time to reconcile differences, Simms remains centered on his theme of love and reconciliation throughout.

At its core *The Golden Christmas* remains today what Simms intended it to be in 1852. It is a gift to Charleston, which to us has become a recorded history of the Carolina Lowcountry's antebellum affluence. Simms's literary portrayal of Charleston and her surrounding plantations is consistent with the antebellum paintings now on display in a number of art museums. Travelling artists who once earned their living in the South by painting plantation studies bear visual witness to the existence of those advanced, polished and self-sufficient communities Simms described in *The Golden Christmas*.

In writing a plantation romance centered on Charleston, Simms was adding his voice to the many who were interpreting the city in antebellum times. The abolitionist Harriet Martineau had already come from England to write the two-volume *Society in America* (1837) in which she misrepresented not only Charleston but also the American South in general. The Swedish authors Bremer and Roos were engaged in jotting down notes on Charleston for their respective travel books. Closer to home were the New England journalists. One, reporting in the *Knickerbocker Magazine* on his 1842 travels to South Carolina, said of Carolinians, "It matters not to them that the spirit of improvement holds the reins of the age. . . . They gaze and admire, perchance, but are still untempted to try its speed or to trust themselves to its destiny."

Today's reader will find that seeing Charleston through the eyes of William Gilmore Simms is more informative than reading what visiting abolitionists and other detractors had to say about a city they neither understood nor loved. Certainly the native-born Simms knew better than these visitors the degree to which the spirit of improvement was making itself felt in Charleston. He demonstrates this spirit at work in *The Golden Christmas*, when he portrays the youth of Charleston in conflict with their elders. Simms also had faith in the Jeffersonian belief that Americans had the good will and the good sense to resolve their own conflicts, especially Americans living in Charleston.

The high culture Simms knew and lovingly portrayed in *The Golden Christmas* was destroyed in the decades which followed the publication of his book. At the peak of its preeminence, the Carolina Lowcountry was invaded, plundered and burned during a war Charlestonians would long refer to as The Late Unpleasantness or The War of Northern Aggression.

In one of his earliest ghost stories "Grayling, A Murder Mystery," Simms worked with the idea that truth comes out in due time. It is my hope that this reissue of *The Golden Christmas* will bring out many truths related to Charleston's rich heritage, much of which was buried in the rubble of The Late Unpleasantness. I firmly believe that this particular ghost of Christmas past conveys some of the wonder that was Christmas in antebellum Charleston.

David Aiken
Charleston

THE GOLDEN CHRISTMAS

THE

GOLDEN CHRISTMAS:

A

CHRONICLE OF ST. JOHN'S, BERKELEY.

COMPILED FROM THE

NOTES OF A BRIEFLESS BARRISTER,

BY THE AUTHOR OF

"THE YEMASSEE," "GUY RIVERS," "KATHARINE WALTON," ETC.

CHARLESTON:
WALKER, RICHARDS AND CO.
1852.

CHARLESTON:

STEAM POWER-PRESS OF WALKER AND JAMES,

101, 103 and 105 East-Bay.

THE GOLDEN CHRISTMAS.

CHAPTER I.

A DOUBTFUL CASE OF LOVE ON THE TAPIS.

IT was during that premature spell of cold weather which we so unseasonably had this year in October,—anticipating our usual winter by a full month or more,—cutting off the cotton crop a fourth, and forcing us into our winter garments long before they were ordered from the tailor,—when, one morning, as I stood shivering before the glass, and clumsily striving, with numbed fingers, to adjust my cravat *à la nœud Gordien*,—my friend, Ned Bulmer, burst into my room, looking as perfect an exquisite as Beau Brummell himself. He was in the gayest clothes and spirits, a thousand times more exhilarated than usual—and Ned is one of those fellows upon whom care sits uneasily, whom, indeed, care seldom *sets upon* at all! He laughed at my shiverings and awkwardness, seized the ends of my handkerchief, and, with the readiest fingers in the world, and in the most perfect taste, adjusted the folds of the cravat, and looped them up into a rose beneath my chin, in the twinkling of an eye, and to my own perfect satisfaction.

"That done," said he,—"what have you now for breakfast?"

A bachelor's breakfast is not uncommonly an extempore performance. I, myself, really knew not what was in the larder, or what my cook was about to provide. But this ignorance occasioned no difficulty. I knew equally well my guest and cook.

"There is doubtless quite enough for two moderate fellows like ourselves. Let us descend to the breakfast room and see."

"I warn you," said he, "I am no moderate fellow at this moment. I am hungry as a Cumanche. I was out late last night at the house of that starched framework of moral buckram, the widow D——e; and got no supper. Her freezing ladyship seems to fancy that she provides well enough when she surfeits every body with her own dignity ; and, though there was a regular party,—a monstrous re-union of town and country cousins,—yet, would you believe it, except the tea service at eight o'clock, cakes and crumpets, and such like unsubstantial stuffs, we got not a mouthful all the evening ! Yet, in momentary expectation of it, every body hung on till twelve o'clock. The case appearing then perfectly desperate, and the stately hostess becoming more freezingly dignified than ever, people began to disappear. The old ladies lingered to the last, and then went off breathing curses, not loud but deep ! Old Mrs. F—— was terribly indignant. I helped her to the carriage. 'Did you,' said she, 'ever see such meanness ? I wonder if she thinks people come to her parties only to see her in her last Parisian dresses ? And that we should stay till twelve o'clock and get nothing after all ! Let her invite me again, and she shall have an answer.' 'Why what will you say ?' said I. 'What will I say ?' said she. 'I'll tell her yes, I'll come, provided she'll allow me to bring my supper with me.'

'And she'll be very sure to do it too,' said I: 'she's just the woman for it.'"

"I shall not quarrel with her if she does. I calculated something on the supper myself, took no tea, and was absolutely famished. I was so hungry that, but for the distance, and my weariness, I should have driven down to Baker's, and surfeited myself upon Yankee oysters. You see now why I am so solicitous on the subject of the sort of breakfast you can provide."

"Faith, Ned," said I, "one might reasonably ask, why, being

so monstrous hungry, you should yet sally forth on an empty stomach! Why didn't you get breakfast at home? Why come to sponge upon a needy bachelor, and without due warning given of the savage character of your appetite?"

"Oh! you penurious monster! You are as stingy as Madame D——e. But, confound you! Do you think it is *your* breakfast, in particular, that I am in search of? Let me quiet your suspicions. Hungry as I am, I have a much more important quest in seeking you, and came as soon as I could, in order to catch you before you should go out this morning. I slept so late, that, when I sprang out of my bed and looked at my watch, I found I hadn't a moment to lose. So I took the chance of securing you and my breakfast by the same operation. Thus am I here and hungry. Are you satisfied?"

"Quite! But what's in the wind now, that you must see me in such a hurry. No quarrel on hand, I trust."

"No! no! Thank God! It is Venus not Mars, at this season of the year, to whom I address my prayers. It is an affair of the heart, not of pistols. But to the point. Have you any engagements to-day? I am in need of you."

"None!" with the natural sigh of a young lawyer, whose desires are more numerous than his clients, and whose hopes are always more magnificent than his fees.

"Good! Then you must serve me, as you can, efficiently. You alone can do it. You must know, then, that Paula Bonneau is in town with her grandmother. They came yesterday, and may leave to-morrow. They are hurried; I don't know why. I heard of them last night at Dame D——e's. They would have been present, and were at first expected; but sent an excuse on the plea of fatigue."

"And did not accordingly—we may suppose—go supperless to bed. But what have I to do in this matter? 'What's Hecuba to

1*

me, or I to Hecuba?' You surely don't design that I should take
Paula off your hands."

"Off my hands, indeed. No! no! *mon ami!* I wish you
rather to assist in putting her into them."

"Humph! not so easy a matter. But how did you hear of
their movements and arrangements?"

"From Monimia Porcher! The dear little creature gave me a
world of news last night, and promises me every assistance. But
she is not a favourite with our grandmother, as you know, and consequently can render me, *directly*, no great assistance. But you
can."

"Prithee, how?"

"I have sent word to Paula by Monimia that I will call upon
her at ten. I know that she and the old lady are to go out shopping at eleven. Now, you will call with me. You are a favourite
with the grandmother, and you are to *keep her off*. I want to get
every possible opportunity; for I am now determined to push the
affair to extremities. I won't take it as I have done. I shall
bring all parties to terms this season, or keep no terms with them
hereafter."

"What! You persist, knowing all your father's anti-Gallican
opinions—his prejudices, inherited for a hundred years!"

"In spite of all! His prejudices are only inherited. They
must be overcome! They are surely nonsensical enough. He
has no right to indulge them at the expense of my happiness."

"To which you really think Paula necessary?"

"Can you doubt! I am a rough dog, you know; but I have
a heart, Dick, as you also know; and I doubt if I could ever feel
such a passion for any other woman as I feel for Paula."

"She is certainly a rare and lovely creature. I am half inclined
to take her myself."

"Don't think of it, you Turk! Content yourself with dreaming of Beatrice Mazyck. I'll help you in that quarter, *mon ami,*

and so will Paula. And *she* can! They are bosom friends, you know."

"But, Ned, her grandmother is quite as hostile to the English Bulmer tribe, as your father is to the Huguenot Bonneaus. You have a double prejudice to overcome."

"Not so! It is the old lady's pride only, that, piqued at the openly avowed prejudices of my family, asserts its dignity by opposition. Let my father once be persuaded to relax, and we shall thaw the old lady. She is devotedly attached to Paula, and, I believe, she thinks well enough of me; and would have no sort of objection, but for the old antipathy to my name."

"You are so sanguine!—Well! I'm ready to help as you require. What is the programme."

"You must secure me opportunities for a long talk with Paula alone. You must keep off the dragon. I am prepared to brave every thing—all my father's prejudices—and will do so, if I can only persuade her to make some corresponding sacrifice for me. I am now tolerably independent. In January, my mother's property comes into my hands ; and, though it does not make me rich, it enables me to snap my fingers in the face of fate ! I am resolved to incur every risk, at all events. Paula, too, is a fearless little creature; and, though wonderfully submissive to the whims of her grandmother, I feel sure that she will not sacrifice herself and me to them in a matter so essential to our mutual happiness. Things are looking rather more favourable than usual. There have been occasional meetings of the two families. The old lady and my father even had a civil conversation at the last tournament; and he has resolved upon a sort of feudal entertainment, this Christmas, which shall bring together the whole neighbourhood,—at least for a day or two. You are to be there: so he requires me to say, and his guest, of course, while in the parish. You must do your endeavour for me while there. It will not be my fault, if the season shall pass without being properly improved. Love has made me somewhat desperate."

"Beware, lest your rashness should lose you all. Your father's prejudices are inveterate."

"I think not. They begin to soften. He begins to feel that he is getting older, and he becomes more amiable accordingly. He talks old prejudices rather than feels them. It is a habit with him now, rather than a feeling. He barks, like the old dog, but the teeth are no longer in capacity to bite. For that matter, his bark was always worse than his bite. What he says of the Huguenots is only what his grandfather said and thought. Without the same animosity, he deems it a sort of family duty, to maintain the old British bull-dog attitude, as if to show that his blood has undergone no deterioration. In respect to Paula, herself, he said, at the last tournament, that she was really a lovely little creature, and regretted that she was of that *soup maigre* French stock. There are sundry other little favourable symptoms which seem to show me that he is growing reasonable and indulgent."

Here, we were signalled to breakfast, and our dialogue, on this subject, was suspended for awhile.

CHAPTER II.

A BACHELOR'S BREAKFAST.

It is not often that our fair readers are admitted to the mysterious domain which entertains a bachelor as its sovereign. They fancy, the dear conceited little creatures, that such a province is a very desolate one. They delude themselves with the vain notion that, without the presence of some one or more of their mischievously precious sex, a house, or garden, is scarcely habitable ; and that man, in such an abode, is perpetually sighing for some such change as the tender sex only can impart. They look upon, as quite orthodox, the language of Mr. Thomas Campbell, who sings—

"The *garden* was a *wild*,
And man, the hermit, sigh'd, till woman *smiled*."

But this is all vanity and delusion. We no where have any testimony that the condition of Adam was thus disconsolate, before Eve was stolen *from* his side, in order that she should steal *to* his side. This is all a mistake. Adam did very well as a gardener, and quite as well as a housekeeper, long before Eve was assigned him as a helpmate, and was very comfortable in his sovereignty alone. We know what evil consequences happened to his housekeeping after she came into it, and what sort of counsellors she entertained. Let it not, therefore, be supposed that we bachelors can not contrive to get on, with our affairs exclusively under our own management. I grant that there is a difference; but the question occurs, 'Is this difference for the worse in our case?' Hardly! There is, confessedly, no such constant putting to rights, as we always find going on in the households of married men. But that is because there is no such *need* of putting to rights. There is previously no such putting to wrongs, in such a household. There, every thing goes on like clockwork. There is less parade, I grant you; but there's no such fuss! Less neatness; but no jarrings with the servants. To the uninitiated eye, things appear in exemplary confusion; but the solitary head of the household can extract order from this confusion at any moment. It is a maze, but not without a plan. You will chafe, because there is a want of neatness; but then our bachelor has quiet. Ah! but you say, how lonesome it looks! But the answer is ready. The bachelor is not, nevertheless, the inhabitant of a solitude. His domain is peopled with pleasant thoughts and sweet visitors, and, if he be a student, with sublime ones. He converses with great minds, unembarrassed by the voices of little ones. He communes with master spirits in antique books. These counsel

and teach him, without ever disputing what he says and thinks.
They fill, and instruct his soul, without vexing his self-esteem.
They bring music to his chamber, without troubling his ears with
noise.   But, you say, he has none of the pleasures which spring
from his communion with children.   You say that the association
with the young keeps the heart young; and you say rightly.   But
the bachelor answers and says—if he has no children of his own,
he sees enough of his neighbours.   They climb his fences, pilfer
his peaches, pelt his dog, and, as Easter approaches, break into his
fowl-yards and carry off his fresh eggs.   Why should he seek for
children of his own, when his neighbours' houses are so prolific?
He could give you a long discourse, in respect to the advantages
of single blessedness,—that is, in the case of *the man.*   In that of
the woman, the affair is more difficult and doubtful.   He is not
prepared to deny that she ought to get married whenever she can
find the proper victim.   To sum up, in brief, he goes and comes
when he pleases, without dreading a feminine authority.   He
takes his breakfast at his own hours, and dines when in the humour, and takes his ease at his inn.   His sleep is undisturbed by
unpleasant fancies.   He is never required to rise at night, no matter how cold the weather, to see that the children are covered, or
to warm the baby's posset.   Never starts with horror, and a chil-
ling shiver, at every scream, lest Young Hopeful, the boy, or
Young Beauty, the girl, has tumbled down stairs, bruizing nose,
or breaking leg or arm; and, if he stays out late o'nights, never
sneaks home, with unmanly terrors, dreading to hear no good of
himself when he gets there.   At night, purring, in grateful reve-
rie, by his fireside, he makes pictures in his ignited coals, which
exhilarate his fancy.   His cat sleeps on the hearth rug, confident
of her master, and never dreading the broomstick of the always
officious chambermaid; and the ancient woman who makes up his
bed, and prepares his breakfast, appears before him like one of

those seeming old hags of the fairy tale who turn out to be princesses and good spirits in homely disguise."

"See now," said I to Ned Bulmer, as Tabitha the cook brought in the breakfast things. "See now, the instance. Tabitha is not comely. Far from it. Tabitha never was comely, even in the days of her youth. Her nose is decidedly African, *prononcé* after the very worst models. Her mouth, a spacious aperture at first, has so constantly worked upon its hinges for fifty-six years, that the lips have lost their elasticity, and the valves remain apart, open in all weathers. Her entire face is of this fashion. She looks like one of the ugly men-women, black and bearded, such as they collect on the heath, amidst thunder and lightning, for the encounter with Macbeth. Yet, at a word, Tabitha will uncover the dishes, and enable us, like the old lady in the fairy legend, to fill our mouths with good things. Such is the bachelor's fairy. Take my word for it, Ned, there's no life like that of a bachelor. Continue one, if you are wise. Paula Bonneau is, no doubt, a delightful little picture of mortality and mischief. But so was Pandora. She has beauty, and sweetness, and many virtues, but she will fill the house with cares, every one of which has a fearful faculty of reduplication. Be a bachelor as long as you can, and when the inevitable fate wills it otherwise, provide yourself with all facilities for dying decently. Coffee, Tabitha."

Such was the rambling exordium which I delivered to my friend, rather with the view of discouraging his anticipations than because I really entertained any such opinions. He answered me in a huff.

"Pshaw! what nonsense is all this! Don't I know that if you could get Beatrice Mazyck to-morrow, you'd change your blessed bachelorhood into the much abused wedlock."

"Fate may do much worse things for me, Ned, I grant you."

"It is some grace in you to admit even so little. But don't you speak again, even in sport, so disrespectfully of the marriage condition. Don't I know the cheerlessness of yours. Talk of your books and ancient philosophers! don't I know that you are frequently in the mood to throw them into the fire; and, even while you sit over it, the reveries which you find so delicious, are those which picture to you another form, of the other gender, sitting opposite you, with eyes smiling in your own, and sweet lips responding at intervals to all the fondest protestations which you can utter. Tabitha, indeed! I verily believe the old creature, though faithful and devoted to you, grows sometimes hateful in your eyes, as reminding you of her sex in the most disagreeable manner;—a manner quite in discord to such fancies as your own thoughts have conjured up. Isn't it so, Tabitha? Isn't Ned sometimes monstrous cross, and sulky to you, only because you haven't some young mistress, Tabitha?"

"I 'spec so, Mass Ned: he sometime mos' sick 'cause he so lonesome yer. I tell um so. I say, wha' for, Mass Dick, you no get you'se'f young wife for make your house comfortable, and keep you company yer, in dis cold winter's a'coming. I 'spec its only 'cause he can't git de pusson he want."

"True, every word of it, Tab! But never you mind. You'll be surprised some day with another sort of person overlooking your housekeeping. What do you think, Tabitha, of Miss Beatrice Mazyck."

"Hush, Ned!"

"She's a mighty fine young pusson, and a purty one too. I don't tink I hab any 'jection to Miss Beatrice."

"Very well! You're an accommodating old lady. She'll be the one, be sure of it. So keep the house in order. You'll be taken by surprise. Then we shall see very different arrangements in the housekeeping here, Tabby. Do you suppose that she'd let Dick lie abed till nine o'clock in the morning, and sit up, smoking and drinking, till midnight?"

"Nebber, in dis world, Mass Ned."

"And, if the power is with her, never in the next, Tabitha. Then, do you think she'd suffer a pack of fellows to be singing through the house at all hours—and such singing, and such songs."

"Nebber guine le' um come, Mass Ned. Him no guine 'courage dis racket yer at all hours. I tell you for true, Mass Ned, dis house, sometime, aint 'spectable for people to lib in. You no know what de young gentlemens do here at night, keeping me up for make coffee for um, sometime mos' tell to-morrow morning."

"It's perfectly shocking, Tabitha. She'll never suffer it."

"Nebber, Mass Ned."

"Then, Tabby, do you think she'd let these tables and chairs be so dusty, that a gentleman can't sit in them without covering his garments with dust as from a meal bag."

"Sure, Mass Ned, I brush off de tables and chairs ebbry morning." And, saying this, the old woman began wiping off chairs and tables with her apron.

"But she'll see it done after a different fashion, Tabitha. She'll have you up at cock crow, old lady, putting the house to rights."

"Hem! I 'spec she will hab for git young sarbant den, for you see Mass Ned, dese old bones have de rheumatiz in dem."

"Not a bit of it, old lady. A young wife has no pity on old bones. She'll make you stir your stumps, if you never did before. She will never part with you, Tabitha. She knows your value. She knows how Dick values you. She will have no other servant than you. You'll have to do everything, Tabby, even to nursing the children. And, between you and her, the old house will grow young again. It will make you happy, I'm, sure, to see it full of young people, and plenty of company, looking quite smart always; always full of bustle and pleasure; every body busy; none idle; not a moment of time, so that, when you lie down at midnight, to rouse up at daylight, you'll sleep as sound as if you were in heaven."

2

"I don't tink, Mass Ned, I kin stan' sich life as dat. De fac'
is, Mass Dick is berry comfortable jist now, as he stan'. He aint
got no trouble. He know me, and I knows him. I don't see
wha' for he want to get wife. I nebber yer him say he's oncom-
ortable."

"Ha! ha! ha! The tune rather changes, Tabitha. But this
house, as it is, is quite too dull for both you and your master.
When Beatrice Mazyck comes home, you'll have music. She will
waken up the day with song, like a bird. She will put the day to
sleep with song. You'll have fine times, Tabby—music, and
dancing, and life and play."

"Wha's people guine do for sleep, Mass Ned, all dis time.
People must hab sleep."

The old woman spoke this sharply. Ned laughed gaily, beck-
oned for another cup of coffee, and the ancient housekeeper was
for the moment dismissed.

"You have effectually cured her of any desire for a mistress,"
said I.

"See how opinion changes," quoth Ned,—"yet Tabitha is no
bad sample of the world at large, white and black. Our opinions
shape themselves wonderfully to suit our selfishness.—Dick, pass
me those waffles."

I suppose there is hardly any need to describe a bachelor's
breakfast. Ours was not a bad one. Coffee and waffles, sardines
and boiled eggs,—to say nothing of a bottle of Sauterne, to which
I confined myself, eschewing coffee in autumn—these were the
chief commodities. The table, I must do Tabitha the justice to
declare, was well spread, with a perfeatly white cloth, and the
edibles served up, well cooked and with a clean and neat arrangement. Edward Bulmer soon satisfied his wolfish appetite, and,
when the things were removed, it was after nine o'clock. His
buggy was already at the door. We adjusted ourselves, and having an hour to consume, went over all the affairs of the parish, of

which he had recently informed himself. Now, as every body knows, St. John's is one of the most polished, hospitable, and intelligent of all the parishes in the low country of South-Carolina ; and the subject, to one like myself who knew it well, and who had not been thither for a long time, was a very attractive one. On Ned's account, also, I was desirous of being well informed in all particulars, that none of the proper clues might be wanting to my hands, while conversing with Paula's granddame. The hour passed rapidly, conning these and other matters, and ten o'clock found us punctually at the entrance of the Mansion House. Our cards were sent in, and, in a few moments, we were in the parlour of that establishment, and in the presence of the fair Paula, and her stately, but excellent granddame, Mrs. ———, or, considering the race, I should probably say, Madame Agnes-Theresa Girardin.

CHAPTER III.

KING-STREET SHOPPING, AND SHARP SHOOTING.

PAULA BONNEAU was as lovely a little brunette as the eye ever rested upon with satisfaction. Her cheek glowed with the warm fires of Southern youth ; her eye flashed like our joyous sunlight; her mouth inspired just the sort of emotion which one feels at seeing a new and most delicious fruit imploring one to feed and be happy ; while her brow, full and lofty, and contrasting with voluminous masses of raven hair, indicated a noble and intellectual nature, which the general expression of her face did not contradict. That was a perfect oval, and of the most perfect symmetry. The nose, by the way, was aquiline, a somewhat curious feature in such a development, but perfectly consistent with the bright eagle-darting glances of her eye. Paula was, indeed, a beauty, but I frankly confess quite too *petite* for my taste. Still, I could admire her, as a beautiful study,—nay, knowing the amiable and superior traits of her heart and character, I could love the little creature also. She was, in truth, a most loveable little being, and, though she did not inspire me with any ardent attachment—perhaps, for the sufficient reason that I had fixed my glances on another object—still, I felt no surprise at the passion with which she stirred the blood in the bosom of my friend.

The contrast between herself, and her stately grand-dame, was prodigious. One could hardly suppose that the two owed their origin to a similar stock. Madame Girardin was tall beyond the ordinary standards of woman, and very disproportionately slender for her height. She was one of those gaunt and ghostly-looking personages, who compel you to think of fierce birds of prey, such as haunt the shores of unknown rivers or oceans, with enormous long limbs, long beaks, red heads, and possibly yellow legs. Her nose was long like her limbs, and tapered down to a point like a spear head. Her lips were thin and compressed. She could not well be said to show her teeth, whatever might be the fierceness of her looks in general. Her eyes were keen and black, her eye brows thick, furzy and pretty well grizzled, while her locks were long, thin, grizzled also, and permitted rather snakily to hang about her temples. The dear old grandmother was decidedly no beauty; but she was noble of spirit, high-toned, and of that sterling virtue and stern character, which constituted so large a portion of our female capital in preceding generations. She had her faults, no doubt, but she was a brave-souled, and generous woman. Her great weakness was her family pride—vanity, perhaps, we should call it—which made her overrate the claims of her own stock, and correspondingly disparage those of most other households. Like many other good people, who have otherwise very good common sense, she really persuaded herself that there was some secret virtue in her blood that made her very unlike, and very superior to other people. Like the Hidalgos, she set a prodigious value upon the genuine *blue* blood—perhaps, she even esteemed hers as of a superior *verdigris* complexion, the result of continued strainings and siftings, through the sixty millions of generations from Adam. Had she been queried on this subject, perhaps she might have admitted a belief that certain angels had been specially designated, at the general dispersion of the human family, at some early period, to take charge of the Girardins, and to see, whenever the sons and daughters were to be wived and husbanded, that none but a *bonâ fidè* first cousin should be found to meet the wants of the parties to be provided. Enough of this. It was her weakness—a little too frequent in our country, where society is required of itself to establish distinctions of *caste*, such as the laws do not recognize, and such as elsewhere depend upon the requisitions of a court. The weaknesses of Madame Girardin, as I have already said, did not prevent her from being a very worthy old lady,—i. e., so long as you forebore treading upon the toes of her genealogy.

Knowing her weaknesses, and forbearing, if not respecting them, I was something of a favourite with the old lady, who received me very cordially. Such also was my reception at the hands of the young one,—possibly, because she knew the part that I was likely to take in promoting the *affaire de cœur* between herself and my friend. But I should not impute this selfishness to her. Paula was a frank, gentle creature, who had no affectations—no pretensions—and was just as sincere and generous as impulsive and unaffected. We had been friends from childhood— her childhood at least—had played a thousand times together in the parish, and I had no reason to doubt the feeling of cordiality which she exhibited when we met. My social position was not such as to outrage the self-esteem of either. The Coopers of the parish—an English cross upon a Huguenot stock,—seem not to have inherited any prejudices of race from either the English or

2*

French side of the house. We had consequently provoked none
of the enmities of either. In the case of our family, the amalgam
of the two had been complete, and we occupied a sort of neutral
place between them, sharing the friendship, in equal degree, of
the descendants of both. Hence, I was, perhaps, an equal favourite of old Major Bulmer, Ned's father, and of Madame Agnes-
Theresa, Paula's grandmother.

But, to our progress. Of course, I took special care of the
grandmother during our morning call. By the most watchful
and—shall I say—judicious solicitude—I kept her busily engaged
on such parish topics as I knew to be most grateful to her pride
and prejudices. I got her so deeply immersed in these matters
that she entirely forget her duenna watchfulness over the two
other persons in the apartment. Of course, I took care not to
look towards them, as they sat together near the piano, at the
opposite side of the parlour, lest I should divert the eyes of the
grandmother in the same direction. And thus we chatted, Ned
making all possible amount of hay during the spell of sunshine
which he enjoyed, and Paula tacitly assisting him by never showing any clouds herself. Time flew apace, and we had consumed
nearly an hour, when the old lady suddenly looked at her watch,
and exclaimed—

" Why, Paula, child, it is almost eleven. What have you been
talking about all this time ?"

The good grandmother, like most other old ladies, never dreamt
that she herself had been doing any talking at all. Paula immediately started, like a guilty little thing, and exclaimed art-
lessly—

" Dear me, mamma, can it be possible."

" Possible, indeed !" responded the grandmother rather sharply.
" You young people seem never to think how time flies. But get
your bonnet, child. Mine is here."

The maiden disappeared for a few moments, glad to do so, for her cheeks betrayed a decided increase of the rich suffusion which owes its fountains to the excited heart. While she was gone, Ned was most profoundly courteous to the ancient lady, and she most courteously cold. When Paula came back, I asked of Madame Agnes-Theresa—

" Do you walk, Madame Girardin."

" Yes ; we have not far to go, only into King-street, where we have some shopping to do."

" If you will suffer me," said I, " I shall be happy to accompany you. I have quite a taste and a knack at shopping."

A most deliberate lie, for which the saints plead, and the heavens pardon me. I know no occupation that more chafes and fatigues me ; but Ned's affairs had rendered my tastes flexible and my conscience obtuse.

" But it will be taking you from your business. You young lawyers, Mr. Cooper, are said to be very ambitious and very close students."

I did not laugh at the old lady's simplicity, though I might have done so ; but answered with corresponding gravity—

" Very true, ma'am, but that is just the reason why we relish a little respite, such as a morning's ramble in King-street promises. Besides, I have really nothing just now to occupy me."

And this said, too, while the Court of Common Pleas was in session. Of course, I did not tell the good lady that I had not a single case on the docket. I suppressed that fact for the honour of the profession, and the credit of the community. The old lady was fond of deference and attention, and, as old ladies are not often so fortunate as to secure the *chaperonage* of handsome young gentlemen, she was not displeased that I should urge upon her my duteous attendance. My services were accepted, and, taking my arm, only looking round to see that Paula did *not* take that of Ned Bulmer, she led the way out of the parlour and into the

street.   From Meeting to King, through Queen-street, was but a
step, and we were soon in our fashionable ladies' thoroughfare.

The day was a bright and mild one, just such as we commonly
experience in November,—cooler and more pleasant than usually
characterizes the present month of October.   The street was
crowded with carriages, and the trottoir with fair and happy
groups all agog with the always grateful excitement—to the
ladies—of seeing one another, and—fancy dresses.   Our country
cousins were encountered at every turning, and, between town and
country, we had to run the gauntlet of old acquaintance, and
often repeated recognition.   It was quite delightful to see how my
dignified and venerable companion met and acknowledged the
salutations of those she knew.   Her demeanour varied with strict
discrimination of the *caste* and quality of each acquaintance.   She
was a sort of social barometer, exactly telling by her manner,
what sort of blood flowed in the veins of each to whom she
bowed or spoke.   To some few she unbent readily, with a spontaneous and unreserved and placid sweetness ; to others she was
starch and buckram personified, and, to not a few, her look was
vinegar and vitriolic acid.   Even where I myself did not know the
parties, personally, I had only to notice her manner as they approached, to find their proper place, high or low, in the social circles of town or country.   Good, old, aristocratic Dame Girardin
was an admirable graduating scale, for determining the qualities
of the stock, and the colour of the blood, in the several candidates
for her notice, as we perambulated our Maiden Lane.   See her in
contact with a person of full flesh—a *parvenu*, not yet denuded of
vigour by the successive intermarriages of cousins for an hundred
years—and the muscles of her face became corrugated like those of
an Egyptian mummy, who had been laid up in lavender leaves
and balsams, since the time of the Ptolomies ;—but, the next
moment, you were confounded to see her melt into sunshine and
zephyr, as she encountered some dried-up, saffron-skinned atomy,

having legibly written on her cheeks, a parchment title to have sate at the board of Methuselah. It was absolutely delightful.

Her comments upon the parties were equally rich and instructive. A fine-looking, cheery lady, the well known and very attractive Mrs. ———, looked out from her carriage window, and smiled and chirrupped to her as she drove slowly by.

"A vulgar creature!" exclaimed my ancient companion—"what a coarse voice,—what a fat vulgar face she has. No delicacy. But how should she have any? She pretends to be somebody now, because she has a little money; but if I were to say what she was—or rather what her grandfather was—I knew him very well, and have bought my negro shoes from him a hundred times. The upstart. Ah!"—with a deep sigh—"every thing degenerates. Lord knows what we will come to at last. It is a hard thing to find any body of pure blood in the city now! Such a mingling of puddles! This trade! This commerce! I declare it's the ruin of the country!"

Here I ventured to interpose a word for the fair woman thus hardly dealt with—one of my own acquaintance, whom I had every reason to esteem;—and I said—

"It's unfortunate, to be sure, that Mrs. ———'s grandfather dealt in negro shoes; but she seems to have got over the misfortune pretty well. She is now every where acknowledged in the best society."

"The more's the pity. Best society, indeed. There are half a dozen circles, calling themselves the best society in Charleston, and don't I know that, in each, they are crowded with *parvenus*—people of yesterday—without any claims to blood or family—descendants of Scotch and Yankee pedlars,—mechanics—shopkeepers—adventurers of all sorts, who have nothing but their impudence and their money—made, heaven knows how—to help them forward."

"But," continued I, "Mrs. ———, is really a very charming

woman—she is very clever, very pretty, and is considered very amiable."

"It's impossible. As for pretty, that, I suppose, is a matter of taste; and I can hardly allow even that. Mere health, and smooth cheeks, and youth, are very far from constituting beauty. Beauty depends upon delicacy, and symmetry, and—blood. As for clever—I suppose you mean she's smart."

"Yes!"

"Smartness is vulgar. Rank and family don't need to be smart. Talent is necessary to poverty, or to inferiority of social position, since it is, perhaps, necessary that there should be something, by way of compensation, given to persons who are poor and without family rank. But wealth, talent and beauty, even—if all combined—can never supply those graces of manner and character, which are the distinguishing qualities of high birth."

"But successive generations in the possession of wealth and talent, my dear madam," I suggested, "must surely result in those excellencies of manner, taste and character, which you properly insist upon as so important."

"Impossible! Let me warn you against any such conclusions," responded the old lady, with a parental shake of the head and finger.

"But," said I, "of course, even the most select stocks in the world, must have had a beginning once, in some of the ordinary necessities of life."

"No, sir; no, Mr. Richard"—almost with severity—"certain families have been always superior, from the beginning! Here now, here comes Colonel ———. He is one of those, whose families were always, beyond dispute, in the highest circles. Ah! the poor gentleman, how feeble he is—see how he walks, as if about falling to pieces."

"Yet he is scarcely more than fifty."

"Ah! he is so wretched. He has no children, and he so longs for a son, and his name will probably die out."

"Yet, he has been thrice married."

"Yes! yes! he first married Mary ——, then her sister Jane, and lastly, her younger sister, Matilda;—and no children."

"All were his cousins, I think?"

"Yes! and Matilda is even now, I hear, a dying woman! I'm sure I pity him from the bottom of my soul. That such a family should become extinct."

"He is now poor, I am told. Has run through his fortune."

"Run through his fortune, Mr. Cooper! I don't like the phrase. He has lived like a gentleman and a prince, and has become impoverished in consequence. He has erred, perhaps, by such extravagant living; but I cannot think severely of a person who has spent it in such a noble style of hospitality. My heart bleeds for him!"

Here the person spoken of approached,—a person well known about town,—one who had wasted his means like a fool, and had not the soul to recover them like a man,—whose ancestors had exhausted the physical vigour of the family by a monstrous succession of intermarriages; and who had consummated the extreme measure of their follies, by himself marrying three cousins in succession. The natural consequence was physical and moral imbecility. The race had perished, and it was, perhaps, just enough that its possessions should disappear also. I confess that I felt but little sympathy for such a person; and as he tottered up to us, and smirked, and smiled, and sniggered, and talked with an inanity corresponding exactly with his character, the pity which his poverty and feebleness might have inspired, was all swallowed up in the scorn which I felt for such equal impotence and vanity.

"Ah! it's melancholy," said the old lady, as he left us; "such a name, such a family, so reduced—reduced to one, and he, you may say, already half in the grave."

I had half a mind to ask the old lady, if she didn't think it would have been preferable had his father married some vigorous young woman of no family at all, and brought up his son to some manly occupation; so that he himself might be now vigorous, with sense enough to marry, in turn, some vigorous young woman, of no family at all; having health all round, numerous children to perpetuate the name, and energies sufficient to preserve the fortune;—but I felt the danger to the cause of Ned Bulmer, of touching upon ground so delicate; and, at this moment, the worthy granddame looked about her for Paula and her companion. In her disquisitions upon the new and vulgar people, and her long talk with the dying Castilian of rare blue blood, she had quite forgotten the young couple. They had enjoyed the field to themselves, and were now not to be seen. The old lady took the alarm. I told her they had probably popt into Kerrison's, and we went back to look for them. There they were, sure enough, Paula looking over silks and velvets—a wilderness of beauty, in the ample world and variety of the accommodating house in question—but with Ned Bulmer close to her side, whispering those oily delights into her ear, with which young lovers are apt to solace themselves and their companions, in this otherwise very cheerless existence. It was evident to me, from the grave face of the damsel, and the conscious one of Ned, that he had done a large amount of haymaking that morning. Whether the old lady suspected the progress which he had made or not, it was not easy to determine. She did not show it, and was soon as much interested in the examination of the various and gorgeous fabrics around her, as any younger person in the establishment,—which, as usual, was crowded like a ball-room. Kerrison's, indeed, is quite a lounge for the ladies;—a place where, if you wish to find your friends and acquaintance, without the trouble of looking them up, you have only to go thither. The dear old grandmother soon found sundry of hers, of town and country, and was again in little while under full sail over the sea of social conversation—one of those admirable seas, by the way, in which no one gets out of his depth. Of course, when Madame Girardin got as deeply as she could amidst the waters, Ned Bulmer resumed his toil upon the meadows at the more sunny and profitable occupation. I loitered at a convenient distance between the duenna and the damsel, contriving, in the most unconscious manner in the world, to interpose as a sort of shield for the protection of the latter from the occasional glances of the former. When Madame seemed to have bathed long enough, in her favourite streams, and turned again to the counter, she found me promptly at her elbow turning over for her inspection piles of changeable silk, chintzes of the finest patterns, shawls and other stuffs, for which my experience in the dry goods business is not sufficient to allow me to recall the proper names. Fancy the dreariness of this employment—reviewing for a mortal hour all sorts of fabrics, coarse and fine, silk and frieze, cloths worthy of a nobleman, and cloths not unworthy of Sambo and Sukey! Verily, friendship required of me great sacrifices that day, and I inwardly swore that Ned should suffer, in a basket of champagne at least, to be sent the very next day to my lodgings. (*Par parenthese*, he did so—and helped me to drink it too!) I even undertook, such was my good nature, to get the good grandmother's orders for groceries supplied—listening patiently to a volume of instructions touching the quality of raisins, citron, almonds, and other matters, all portending cakes, pies, puddings, and other Christmas essentials and essences. But this aside.

From Kerrison's we sauntered off to Lambert's and Calder's, the old lady being sworn to a new tapestry carpet, and being very choice about colours and figures. The choice was made at last, and after picking up some rings, chains, and other pretty trinkets at Hayden's, intended for Christmas presents, dear little Paula recollected that she required books; so we went to Russell's. Here

3

the stately grandmama, trained in the stiff old schools, recoiled with a feeling akin to horror, as her eye rested on the exquisite and elaborate busts of Psyche and the Greek Slave. I couldn't persuade her to a second look at them.

"Such shows," said she, "would not have been permitted in my day. Powers, indeed! He must be a very bad person. But, I have said already, I see what we're coming to. The good old stocks die out, and every thing degenerates. Loose morals, vulgar fashions, bad manners, and gross, coarse, nameless people, of whom nobody even heard ten years ago."

A large picture in front arrested her eye. Certain chubby angels, suspended in air, were waiting for the escaping soul of a dying martyr. The old lady seemed quite distressed about the angels. Her criticism would, no doubt, have greatly afflicted the artist.

"Why," said she, "they look as if they were going to tumble upon the heads of the people. And well they may; for the painter has made them so fat and vulgar that no wings in the world can keep them up. As if an angel should have fatness. They look as if they fed upon pork and sausages. It's very shocking— very vulgar. Why, Paula, those angels look for all the world like the great-checked, troublesome fat boys of old Cargus,—only he don't let em go quite so bare in cold weather."

Russell nearly fainted at this criticism, but he did not despair of the old lady, and modestly suggested that he could show her something which he fancied would please her better.

"Only step back here, ma'am," said he in his most courteous manner. But the dear old Castilian grandmama was not to be inveigled even by the profound bow and graceful smile of our courtly Bibliopolist.

"No! sir!" quoth she with stately courtesy—"I thank you; I have seen enough—quite enough. Such things are not grateful to my eyes. I am only sorry that they should please any eyes."

And she looked as if she were about to add—"I have lived only too long." And she nodded her head slowly several times, as if over the wickedness of the modern Nineveh,—by which, of course, you must understand, our poor little city of Charleston. Paula was less sensitive, and of course more sinful. She looked with eager eyes at the beautiful busts, hung upon the Psyche, much to the disquiet of grandmama, even contemplated the picture of the hideous looking saint, and the vulgarly fat little angels, and, following Russell into the back room was startled into admiration by the exquisite ideal of the Escaping Soul. I can't say that she was much impressed by the Transfiguration—certainly not with the tributary scene at the foot of the mountain. But we must stop. It was three o'clock before we had finished the shopping ramble through King-street. When we left the ladies again at the Mansion House, Ned Bulmer was quite in high spirits, and full of commendations.

" You did the thing handsomely, Dick, and I flatter myself I have done the thing handsomely too. Paula does not promise me positively to run up the flag of independence ; but she has suffered me to see that she will never compel me to commit matrimony with any body else, or suicide for the want of her. And now for dinner. You take your soup with me to-day, of course.

CHAPTER IV.

THE PARISH.—THE BULMER BARONY.

OUR scene now changes from town to country—from St. Philip's and St. Michael's to St. John's, surnamed of Berkeley. Dame Agnes-Theresa and Paula Bonneau had taken their departure from Charleston, the second day after our shopping expedition through

King-street. I had seen them that night and the next, on both occasions accompanied by Ned Bulmer. I am happy to inform my pleasant public that nothing transpired during those two visits to undo the favourable results which have been already reported. By dint of the utmost vigilance and solicitude, I contrived to steer wide of the morbid sensibilities of our grandmother, or so to handle them as to leave her as amiably soothed as under the passes of a scientific magnetizer. Miss Martineau could not have operated more admirably for the recovery of her favourite dun cow, which all the doctors had given up. The auspices thus favourable, we beheld their departure for the country with confident anticipations, and after the lapse of a week Ned Bulmer followed them. Not, be it remembered, that he proceeded to visit them at Rougemont, the plantation seat of the Bonneau family for a hundred years—so called, because the house was erected on a red clay bank,—but that he went into the same parish, and somewhat in the immediate neighbourhood, trusting to the chapter of accidents, —being always in the way—for an occasional meeting with the lovely Paula. As for going straight to Rougemont, even for a morning call, that was a thing impossible. The good old grandmother, hospitable and courtly as she was, had never honoured him with the slighest intimation that his presence there would be agreeable. She was somewhat justified in this treatment, according to parish opinion, by the long feud which had existed between the Bulmer and Bonneau families. Ned was unfortunate in his operations, and baffled in all his plans and hopes. It so happened that he never met with Paula, nor could he contrive any mode of communicating with her. The consequence was, that after fruitless experiments for ten days, he wrote to urge my early coming up. As a strong inducement to me to anticipate the period which I had assigned for my visit, he advised me of the return of Beatrice Mazyck from the mountains. He knew my weakness with regard to this young lady, and, though he knew my doubts of

success, and could himself hold out no encouragements, his selfish
desires prompted him to counsel me to hurry up and look also to
the chapter of chances for those prospects which he could not
base upon reasonable probabilities. Was it friendship, or my own
passion, that moved me to an instant compliance with his request?
The reader is permitted to suppose just which he pleases. I pushed for the parish in three days after receiving his letter, leaving
my law office in the hands of my young friend A—— T——;
who so happily divides himself between Law and Poesy, without
having the slightest misgivings of the jealousy of either mistress.
The legal control of my bachelor household was yielded to Tabitha, my cook,—who, since the awkward hints of Ned Bulmer, had
taken frequent occasions to assure me that the peace of my house
was secure only so long as it was that of a bachelor.

The Bulmer Barony—for old Bulmer, great-great-grandfather to
Ned, had been one of the Barons of Carolina, when, under the
fundamental constitutions ascribed to Locke, the province had a
nobility of its own—was still a splendid estate, though considerably cut down from its old dimensions of twenty-thousand acres.
I suppose the "Barony," now, includes little more than four thousand. Still, it was a property for a prince, and the present in-
cumbent, Major Marmaduke Bulmer, was accounted one of the
wealthiest of our landholders. He owned some three hundred
slaves, of whom half the number, perhaps, were *workers.* Ned's
own property, in right of his mother, was a decent beginning for a
prudent man, and he was looking about for the purchase of a
small plantation in the neighbourhood on which to settle, as soon as
his negroes came under his own control. At the "Barony" I
was received with such a welcome, as none knows better how to
accord than the Carolina gentleman of the old school. Major Bulmer had been trained in this school, which, by the way, in the
low country parishes, was of two classes. There was an English
and a French class. The one was distinguished by frankness, the

3*

other by propriety;—the former was rough and impulsive, the latter scrupulous and delicate ; the former was apt to storm, occasionally, the latter to sneer and indulge in sarcasm ; the former was loud and eager ; the latter was tinctured with propriety which sometimes became formality.   In process of time, the two schools modified each other ; at all times, they were equally hospitable and generous : fond of display, scorning meanness, and, accordingly, too frequently sacrificing the substantial securities of life, for the more attractive enjoyments of society.   This will suffice to give an idea of the general characteristics of the two classes.   Major Bulmer was not an unfair specimen of the former.   He did not belong to the modern mincing school of the English, which has somewhat impaired its manners by graftings from the Continent which sit but awkwardly on the sturdy old Anglo-Norman stock. He was not a nice, staid, marvellously measured old gentleman, who said "how nice !" when he was delighted with any thing, and hemmed and hawed over a sentence, measuring every word as if he dreaded lest he should commit a lapse in grammar.   On the contrary he was apt to blurt out the words just as they came uppermost, as if perfectly assured that he could say nothing amiss. So again, instead of the low, subdued, almost whispered tones which the modern fine gentleman of England affects, he was apt to be somewhat loud and voluminous—boisterous, perhaps—when a little excited, and at all times sending out his utterances with a sort of mountain torrent impulse.   In a passion, his voice was a sort of cross between the roar of a young lion, and the scream of an eagle darting after its prey.

But, the reader must not suppose that Major Bulmer was a sort of American Squire Western.   He was no rough, ungainly, sputtering, swaggering, untrained, untrimmed north country squire, bull-headedly bolting into the circle, and storming and splurging through it, wig streaming and cudgel flourishing on every hand. The Major was a man of force and impulse, but he was a man of dignity also. His character was bold and salient—his nature demanded it—but it had been trained, and in not a bad school. It had the sort of polish which was at once natural to, and sufficient for it, and his impulse was not without its grace, and his vehemence was not wanting in the necessary forbearance. No doubt, he sometimes shocked very weak nerves; and, knowing that, he was not apt to force his way into sick chambers. If the invalid sensibility came in his way, it was at its own peril. So much for the Major's *morale*. His *personnel* was like his moral. He was large, well made, erect at sixty, with full rosy cheeks, lively blue eyes, a frosty pow, but a lofty one, and he carried himself like a mountain hunter. On horseback, he looked like a natural captain of cavalry, and, I have no doubt he would have led a charge such as would have made Marshal Ney clap hands in approbation.

The Major met me at the porch of "The Barony," and took me by the shoulders, instead of by the hands.

"What, Dick, "said he, "what, the devil! You are letting hard study and the law kill you up. You are as thin as a cypress pole, and look quite as melancholy. You are pale, wan, and quite unlike what you were two years ago. Then, you could have stood a wrestle with any of us,—now,—deuce take me Dick, if I can't throw you myself."

And he seemed half disposed to try the experiment.

"But this Christmas in the parish will bring you up again. You must recruit. You must throw those law books to the devil. No man has a right to pursue any study or profession which impairs manhood. Manhood, Dick, is the first of virtues. It includes, it implies them all. Strength, health and courage,—these are the first necessities—without these I would'nt give a fig for any virtue. It could'nt be useful without it, and a stagnant virtue might as well be a vice for all the benefit it does society."

I report the Major literally. His speech will show the reader the sort of character with whom he has to deal. I need not say that I was received at "The Barony," as if I had been one of the household. Miss Janet Bulmer, the maiden sister of the Major, a calm, quiet, sensible, and rather pretty antique—she certainly had been pretty, and, by the way, had been crossed in love—welcomed me as affectionately as if I had been her own son. She was the Major's housekeeper, shared some of his characteristics, if not his prejudices, but was subdued even to meekness in her demeanour. Not that she had lost her spirit; but its exercise seldom suffered provocation. She rescued me from the clutches of her brother, and conducted me to my chamber, in what was called the garden wing of the establishment. It was near sunset when I arrived, and Ned Bulmer was absent; no one knew whither. He had gone out on horseback; I suspected in what direction. I was busy at the toilet, adjusting myself for presentation at supper, when he burst into the room, with a cry of joy and welcome. He had a great deal to say, but the report was not favourable. He had not yet been able to meet with Paula.

"But now that you are come, my dear fellow, you will call upon the old lady, and convey the necessary message to the young one."

All of which I promised. We were yet busy in details when Zack, the most courtly negro that ever wore gentleman's livery, made his appearance.

"Happy to see you, Mr. Richard,—very happy, sir ;—not looking so well as in old times, Mr. Richard ;—hope you'll improve, sir, at the Barony. Mr. Ned,—Miss Janet says—supper's on table, gentlemen."

Stately, courteous, deliberate, respectful, considerate, proper, reserved, always satisfactory, Zacharias! You are a treasure in any gentleman's household! We promptly obeyed the summons of Aunt Janet—for so I had long been accustomed to call her, in the language of my friend.

CHAPTER V.

SUPPER AND PHILOSOPHY.

IF, dear reader, you have been one of those luckless earthlings to whom an indulgent providence has never permitted the enjoyment of the hospitalities of a Southern plantation, the proprietors of which have been trained to good performances, by long practice, under generous tuition, derived from the habits, customs, manners, tastes and wealth of long time ago,—I can only pity your ignorance, for, it is not possible, in the brief space allotted to me in this narrative, to undertake to cure it. You must gather up from incidental suggestions and remarks, as I proceed, what faint notion I may thus afford you, of the thousand nameless peculiarities which so gratefully distinguish social life in the regions through which we ramble together. It is not pretended, mark me, that in this respect we have undergone no changes. Far from it. The last thirty years have done much to render traditional, in many quarters, those graces of hospitality which constituted the great charm of our old plantations ; and, in particular, to lose for us the solid advantages of an English training and education, as it was taught eighty years ago to our planters in Europe, without giving to their descendants any corresponding equivalent for it. Still there are tokens and trophies of the past, making dear and holy certain ancient homesteads—an atmosphere of the venerably sweet in the antique, the spells of which have not entirely passed away. But these tokens no longer exhibit the usual vitality, though they retain the familiar form. Their traces may be likened to the withered rose leaves in your old cabinet, that still faintly appeal to the senses, but rather recall what they cannot restore, and pain you by the contrasts they force upon you, rather than compensate you by their still lingering sweetness.

It was the pride and passion of Major Bulmer,—who was fully conscious of the changes going on in the country,—that "Bulmer
Barony" should be the last to surrender those social virtues which
constituted the rare excellence of our old plantation life in the
South.

His home was a venerable brick mansion, after the old English
fashion in most respects,—a great square fabric, with wings. The
passage-way or hall was spacious, and the massive stair-flight that
ascended from it, was of mahogany of the most solid fabric. No
miserable veneering was the broad plate, and the elaborate mould-
ing. This great house was always kept in thorough repair ;—
not looking fresh and shiny, with paint and plaster, and green
blinds,—but kept whole,—no decay suffered,—no sign of decay,
even though the ivy was suffered to creep and clamber, greening
the whole north wall, leaving but narrow space for the windows
even, and stretching round and hanging over the corners of the
house on the east and west. Not a service or a servant was lessened, or cut off from the establishment as it was known in the
days of his grandfather. The butler, the porter, the waiters, the
out-riders, the post-boy,—all were the same. He still drove his
coach and four, though he permitted himself a buggy with four
seats and driven by a pair, occasionally giving it a curse, not because it did not exactly please him, but because it was an innovation. Breakfast, dinner, lunch, supper—all after the old fashion—
recurred ever at the same period. The cook had been so regulated that she herself had become a first rate time-piece. It was
surprising how admirably her time corresponded with that of the
hall clock, which was always kept in proper order. Then, there
could be no possible change in the character of the dishes. These
were rigidly old English,—nay, almost Saxon in their solidity.
"None of your French kickshows for me," quoth the Major, when
his son spoke of *pâté de foiè gras*. What ! eat the liver complaint ! and that of a goose too. May I swallow my own liver

first. No! Ned! none of that nonsense, boy. It is quite enough to sicken me to see you with that d—d swallow-tailed republican French coat, which you properly call a *Lamartine*."

"Why, father, it is a mere elaboration of an English shooting jacket."

"Nonsense! You are speaking of the modern English, who are nothing but continental apes and asses. The real old English, before they became corrupted with their paltry affectations, would have scorned such a popinjay fashion. At all events, if you will wear such a monstrosity, and disfigure an otherwise good person, you are at liberty to do so, but by —— no French diseases shall be employed as a substitute for wholesome human food, at the Barony, while I am the master of it."

Accordingly, the supper table of Major Bulmer exhibited no imported meats, unless we include in this category a delicious Buffalo tongue, of which I devoured more than a reasonable man's proportion. Some excellent stuffed beef, part of a round from dinner, a ham into which the first incisions were that day made, some cold mutton, which I contend to be a specially good thing in spite of Goldsmith's sneering reference, (in Retaliation,) and a variety besides, made the table literally to groan under its burden; and the reader will suppose a corresponding variety of bread stuffs and cakes, jellies and other matters. Ask Major Bulmer, on the subject, and he would readily admit the doubtful taste of such arrangement and display. "But," says he, "it is the old custom. I inherited it—it is sacred as the practice of my ancestors,—and in these days of democracy, which threaten to turn the world upside down, in which old things are to become new, I do not feel myself at liberty to question the propriety of the few antique fashions which I am permitted to retain. I prefer to incur the reproach of a deficient taste to that of a failing veneration."

We did ample justice to the provisions—our appetite suffering no censure from taste in respect to the arrangements of the table.

After supper we adjourned to the library,—Major Bulmer improving, by the way, upon his grandfather, having contrived to make a handsome collection of some three thousand volumes, all in solid *English* bindings (done in New-York) and in massive cases, manufactured out of our native forest growth. These, I am happy to say, issued from the workshops of Charleston. Here, with floor finely carpeted, books around us for every temper, a rousing fire of oak and hickory in the ample fireplace, and each of us disposed in great rocking chairs, we meditated through the media of the best Rio Hondos—the Major excepted—who preferred to send up the smokes of Indian sacrifice, from a native clay pipe, which he had bought thirty years before from a Catawba.

"Life!" quoth the Major,—"Life!"—that was all. The smoke did the rest, and each of us instinctively thought of vapour.

"Yes, life is not such a bad thing!" continued the Major. "Nay! give a man enough to go upon, and life is rather a good thing in its way. Indeed, I am not sure but I would rather live than not. Somehow, I get on very well. I make good crops, and I have a good appetite. I can back a horse against a regiment, and I have a taste for Madeira. Yet I have had troubles, and cares, and anxieties. That son, Dick, is one of my anxieties. I want to see the fellow married."

"I suspect," said I, "that he would like to see himself married."

"No, indeed!" quoth the Major quickly. "Why, the d——l, should he wish to be married! What will marriage do for such a fellow. He is quite too young, yet, to understand its importance. He is too unsettled! He must sow his wild oats first."

"He wants to settle;—and, as for sowing his wild oats, Major, I see no reason why he should not sow them in his own grounds."

"Every chap, now-a-days," responded the Major, "before he fairly chips the shell, wants to settle himself as his own master. Ned has the same foolish hankerings. He talks of buying and planting. Why not plant with me?"

"But you, sir, did not plant with your own father. You set up for yourself, if I remember rightly, before you came of age ;" said Ned, with a chuckle, thinking he had caught the old man between the ribs.

"So I did," said he, "and lost by it. I lost, God knows how, eleven thousand dollars in three years."

"That was because you were so extravagant," quoth Ned irreverently. "Were you to follow my example now."

"Get out, you young rascal! Follow your example! You are looking at that place of old Gendron: but you could never make anything there. It was worn out forty years ago."

"I don't think it was ever worn at all," answered Ned—"I doubt if it was ever ploughed fairly in its life. The surface was only scratched in those days. The good soil yet lies below, and can bring first rate cotton under good cultivation."

"And who made you a planter? What sort of cultivation would you give it, do you think? Do you suppose I would trust you with a crop of mine? Don't I know what will come of your setting up for yourself? In six months you'll be coming to me for money. In a year I shall have to step forward and assume your responsibilities to the tune of two or three thousand dollars, as I did only a year ago."

"Well, father, you'll do it?"

"Will I, then? Perhaps—for I'm too indulgent to you by a long shot, and have been ever since I broke your head with that hickory—"

"Certainly, a decided proof of your indulgence!" cried Ned, with a laugh.

"So it was, for you deserved to have not only your head but every bone in your body broken; but when, in my passion I knocked you down and your blood flooded my best carpet, I thought I had killed you,—as if it were possible to kill such a fellow by any hurt done to the head—and since then a proper con-

4

sideration of my own weight of arm and anger, have made me forbear utterly, until now drubbing would do you no service. You are ruined, I am afraid, for any future use."

"A wife will cure him, Major;" said I.

"And perhaps punish him more effectually than anything I can do; and I shouldn't object provided he could get the right one. But there, again, he is not disposed to do as I want him. He has a hankering after that pretty little Frenchified huzzy, Paula Bonneau, and thinks I don't see—and don't suspect. Answer honestly now, Ned Bulmer, is it not true what I say?"

"I own the soft impeachment, sir;" was the quiet response of Ned, lighting a fresh cigar, and reversing the position of his crossed legs.

"You own—and what a d——d mincing phrase is that. Do you suppose it proper because it *is* taken from Shakspeare. You own it! Well, sir, and why do you suffer yourself to hanker after such a woman as that? Not a woman in fact—a mere child—a doll—a pretty plaything—more like a breast pin than a woman—a very pretty cut Italian cameo, sir; but not fit for a wife. What sort of children, sir, do you suppose such a woman can bring you? Such as will do credit to the name of your family—to the State—able to wield a broad-sword—able to command respect and preside with state and dignity in a parlour, or at a dinner table! Besides, Ned, she's French, and we are English, and for a hundred years there has been an antipathy between our two families!"

"High time to heal it, father;" said Ned, flushed and firing up. "Don't speak unkindly, sir, of Paula Bonneau. You know, sir, it is wrong—you wrong her as a lady, young, innocent, intelligent, of good family, and very beautiful. You wrong yourself as a gentleman, boastful of family, so to speak;—and you know it—and feel it, sir. If Paula is *petite*, as I allow, she is not the less worthy to be the wife of any man, nor will she fail to command respect any where. There's no lady in the parish of better manners, more dignified and amiable, polished and unaffected. As for these old family antipathies and grudges, I do think, sir, that it's a disgrace to common sense that you should entertain them. What if she has French blood in her veins? So have half the English, and the best half too. Your Normans who conquered England infused into it all the vitality that made the race great. All that their descendants have of the noble and the conquering came from the Norman side of the house. The Saxon was a sullen boor, whose sole virtue was his dogged bull-dog tenacity. But the chivalry, the enterprise, the lofty adventure, and the superior tastes, were borrowed from the Normans. Your own family, sir was originally Norman, and you yourself, had you lived three hun dred years ago, might have been proud of your French tongue at an English court. The fact is, sir, you too much underrate our family, its antiquity no less than its character, in dating only from the prejudices of your great-great-grandsire in America. It was in his ignorance of his own origin that he imbibed those prejudi ces, and from his personal rivalries with old Philip Bonneau. It happened unfortunately that his son had a French rival in Paul Bonneau, the son of Philip ; and his son again, in your father found an antagonist in the younger Philip. But you, sir, have no such rival, and why you should, discrediting all gallantry, make a woman, a girl, the object of your antipathy, simply to perpetuate the silly personal prejudices of your ancestors, neither justice, nor generosity, nor common sense, can well see! I protest, sir, it is positively a reproach to your manhood that you should thus reli giously maintain an antipathy, when its object is a sweet, young, artless, and unoffending woman !"

The Major was taken all aback.

"Take breath, Ned, take breath,—or let me breathe a little. Well, sir, have you done ?"

"Done !"

" By the powers, Dick Cooper, did you ever hear a father so be-rated by a son!"

" Really, sir, he proves his legitimacy by the close resemblance of his style to your own."

" Good!—and now Master Edward Bulmer do you suppose that I would not gladly welcome any man-antagonist of the Bonneau family?"

" Nobody suspects you of fear, sir; but courage in the encounter with an armed man, and an equal, is not the sole proof of manliness. The courage, sir, which is just and magnanimous, and which shrinks from the idea of wrong-doing, as from death and shame, is the best proof that one can give of a true nobility. How, sir, with your general sense of what is right—with your pride and sense of honour,—can you reconcile it to yourself to speak sneeringly and scornfully of such a pure, sweet, gentle creature as Paula Bonneau—one who has never wronged you—one, too, whom you know to be the object of the most earnest attachment of your son."

The Major was disquieted. Ned had caught him tripping. He knocked the ashes out of his pipe—put fresh tobacco in—knocked that out also—then stuck the empty pipe into his mouth, and began drawing and puffing vigorously. Ned, meanwhile, had risen, and was taking long strides across the floor. The old man, at length, recovered his tone. He felt the home truths which he had heard, and was manly enough to acknowledge them. He sprang to his feet, with the elasticity of a boy of eighteen.

" Ned's right," said he to me, " after all. He's rough, but he's right. Ned, my son, forgive me. I have wounded you more sorely than I meant."

His arms were extended, and the son rushed into them. For a moment the Major clasped him closely to his bosom. He was proud of his boy—his only—he knew his real nobleness of character, and he felt how much he had outraged it. I felt my eyes suffused at the picture.

" You are right, Ned ; but do me not the injustice to suppose that I meant any wrong to Paula Bonneau. She is a good girl, I verily believe, and a pretty one, I am willing to admit—but, Ned, for all that, look you,—you shall never marry her with my consent. There—enough ! Good night, boys."

Thus saying, the Major hurried off, evidently anxious to avoid any more words.

" Something gained," said I.

" You think so ?"

" Decidedly."

" Yet, you heard his last words ?"

" It doesn't matter ! With a magnanimous nature, the conviction that it has wantonly done a wrong to another, and the desire to repair it, lead always one or more steps beyond. I should not be surprised if Paula Bonneau grows into favour after a while."

" Heaven grant it ; but you are tired. Let us to bed."

CHAPTER VI.

OUR AFFAIRS BECOME MUCH COMPLICATED.

NED BULMER was too eager and anxious about his *affaire du cœur* to give me much respite. His buggy was at the door soon after breakfast the next morning.

" Whither"—asked the Major of his son,—" whither are you going to carry Richard to-day ? Certainly, there is nothing so important as to deny him one day's rest when he gets here."

" I want him to go with me and see this place of Gendron's I am willing to take his opinion of the lands."

4*

"Why, what the deuce can a lawyer know of lands?"

"I shall want him, possibly, to look into the titles and draw up the papers. And as he is something of a surveyor, he can help me to find the lines."

Aunt Janet smiled quietly and whispered to me—"see that you do not trespass upon the lands of Madame Girardin."

I saw that our proceedings were no mystery to her, and guessed that she was not unfriendly to Ned's passion. The Major growled meanwhile, and, at length, said—

"Don't be persuaded any where at present, boys, for we must get up a hunt to-morrow. Bryce tells me that there is a fine old buck that haunts the wood down by the Andrew's bottom field; he saw fresh tracks only this morning. If we turn out early to-morrow, we can start him, and, perhaps, others. At all events, I am for trying. We will see if you youngsters can draw as fine a sight, and pull as quick a trigger, as the old man of sixty."

We promised, and the impatient Ned scored, with a flourish, the brown sides of his bay, sending him forward at a fast city trot, which took us to Gendron's—about five miles—in half an hour. Here we drew up and went into the house which was in charge of the overseer. But here we did not linger. After we had got a draught of cold water and had a little chat with the overseer, Ned thrust into my hands a morsel of a billet which he had prepared before we left "the Barony," which had no address, but was meant for Paula.

"Take the buggy and boy, old fellow, and visit your friend Madame Agnes-Theresa. It is a mile round to the entrance, but the estates join, and—do you see yonder pine woods? They are about eight hundred yards from this spot, but only two hundred from the house at Rougemont. My note says only that I shall be there, and if you can entertain the old lady, so that the young one can make her escape unseen, I am in hopes that she will suffer

me to entertain her there for a season. Only keep the grandmother quiet for a good half hour."

I was successful ; being so fortunate as to find Paula alone in
the drawing-room. I gave her the note, which she was able to
read and conceal from the grandmother. I found the old lady in
the best of humours, quite satisfied with her own purchases in the
city, and particularly pleased with those which I had selected for
her. Upon the raisins, crushed sugar, and almonds, she was especially eloquent, and was graciously pleased to assure me—to my
horror—that hereafter she should employ me to make all her purchases of this nature. My judgment was so highly extolled in
this matter, that I trembled lest she should conclude by proposing
to invest a few thousands, and to go into the grocery business
with me. While she talked, Paula disappeared. Of course, I
encouraged the eloquence of the grandmother. I knew the topics
to provoke it ; but the reader has already had a sufficient sample
of them, and I will not require him to partake of my annoyances.
I was patient, and held on for nearly an hour, until the sweet face
of pretty Paula once more lightened the parlour. Of course, I
had something to say to her, interrupted, however, by the grandmother, who sharply rebuked her for leaving me during the whole
time of my visit. Paula looked to me with the sweetest gravity
in the world, and made the most gracefully evasive apology, which
I perfectly understood, though it was by no means satisfactory to
Madame Girardin. Invitations from both of them, to renew my
visit, dine, and spend the day, were gratefully acknowledged, and,
shaking affectionate hands, I took my departure.

I found Ned Bulmer rather under a cloud. The interview between himself and Paula, under those famous and friendly pines,
had not been quite satisfactory to his ardent and impetuous nature.
Paula entertained some natural feminine scruples at an intercourse
not only secretly carried on, but notoriously against the desires of

both their parents. The little creature had shown herself quite chary and somewhat sad.

"I urged upon her," said Ned, "all that I could in the way of argument to convince her that there was a natural limit to parental rights—that parents had no right to oppose their own mere antipathies to the sympathies of others—that, to indulge these antipathies at the expense of our affections, was a gross and unfeeling injustice—that the right of the parent simply consisted in being assured of the morals and the character of the parties concerned—perhaps, to see, farther, that the means of life were at their command. Beyond this, I contended, that any attempt at authority was usurpation. I urged upon her, in the event of our parents continuing to refuse, that we should marry without regard to their objections. To this, the dear girl positively objected. This roused me a little, and I showed some temper. Then she wept bitterly and called me unkind,—and I—would you believe it, Dick, I wept too,—I suppose for sympathy, and then she was more distressed than ever. The tears of a man, to a woman, are certainly very awful, or very ridiculous. They either show great weakness, or great suffering. Certainly, when Paula saw the drops on my cheek she was positively terrified. But, she was firm still. She would consent to nothing. Dick,—I half doubt if she loves me."

"Pooh! pooh! you are unreasonable. I don't see what more you could require. She gives you the highest proof of love she can,—and you expect her to tear herself away, in defiance, from her only kinswoman—she who has trained her, protected her, been to her a mother. Nonsense! you are too fast! Patience, we must work upon the rock with water. Time! time, man! That is all that you want. The game is more than half won when the lady herself is willing."

"But, I see no progress."

"That is because you only see through the medium of your impatient desires. Time, I say! That is what you require."

We looked about the Gendron plantation of course, which Ned was really disposed to buy, and I gave my opinion in concurrence with his.   This task done, we drove to the " Barony," and got in in good time for dinner.   There were several guests, several old friends, parishioners, and a couple of strangers.   The dining-saloon was a large one, and a noble board was spread.   The supplies of such a board in the South need no recital.   But I may mention that Major Bulmer was famous for his muttons, and he had a choice specimen on table.   The Madeira of rare old vintage circulated freely, and there was no deficiency in the dessert.   When the ladies had retired, and we had finished a bumper or two, we adjourned to the library, where we rather drowsed and dawdled away the remnant of the afternoon than conversed.   We did not return to the supper table, but coffee was brought in to us where we sate, and after a while the guests departed, leaving me pledged to several houses in the neighbourhood, for dinner in some, and lodging and a long visit in others.   When they were all gone, the Major brought up the subject of the Gendron estate.

"Well, what think you of the tract?"—this to me.

"There is a good deal of uncleared land, pretty heavily timbered."

"Only five or six hundred acres, I think."

"But oak and hickory."

"Yes; but not remarkable. Light, Dick, very light, and sandy."

"Better than you think for.   There is also some good pine land too."

"Not much I fancy.   You, perhaps, confounded with it that of the old French woman, Girardin, alongside of it.   By the way, did you think to go and see her.   She is an old friend of *your* family, at least, and very exacting.   If you did not call upon her, and she hears of you in the neighbourhood, you are out of her books forever."

"I did call.   I left Ned at Gendron's, and went over and saw

the ladies. Madame Girardin and myself confabulated for an hour.
I saw her in the city, and have fortunately found favour in her
sight by a successful selection of groceries.   I so pleased her, that,
to my horror, she assures me I shall always be permitted to choose
her groceries,—the sugars, raisins, citron, almonds, &c., in particular."

"Ha! ha! ha!   What a creature!   Yet she has some good
points.   She is a fast friend, and hates like the devil!   And I call
these the inevitable companion-virtues, as clearly indispensable to
each other as good and evil in the world.   What a bunch of prejudices she is, tied up like a bundle of vipers in a hole throughout
the winter.   I believe she hates every thing English."

I smiled in my sleeve, and was about to add,—" as you hate
every thing French,"—but in truth, Major Bulmer's prejudices did
not amount to hates.   There was really no passion in them at all.
He had simply imbibed certain habits of speech,—perhaps certain
prescriptive thoughts—nay, notions would be the better word—and
simply stuck to them as persons of insulated life will naturally do,
wanting that attrition of intellectual society which rubs off salient angles, and deforming protuberances.   It struck me, however,
while thinking thus indulgently of the Major's prejudices, that it
might be no bad policy to show up those of Madame Girardin in
their true colours.   His dislike of her would perhaps enable him
to see how equally loathsome and ridiculous is the indulgence of
a blind, insane hostility to things and persons of whom, and which,
we really know no evil.   Accordingly, I was at pains to report the
conversation which was had between the old lady and myself in
our shopping expedition, in which she emptied so freely her bag
of gall upon trade and tradesmen, parvenus and clever people.   I
did not spare her, you may be sure, and made the portrait as fan-
tastically true as possible.   The Major laughed and clapped his
hands delightedly.

" What an atrocious old monster.   Who ever heard the like?

To think favourably of such a meanspirited, unperforming, snivelling creature as ——, to think indulgently even of such a· base fardel of inanities, seems to me an equal outrage upon decency and common sense; but to denounce commerce, which has made England queen of the seas, mistress of the destinies of nations, which carries civilization and art wherever it goes, which stirs up and inspirits intellect, endows the animal with soul, and informs the clay with energy and action. What a diabolical old fool. But she hates commerce because it is so thoroughly English! That's it! And yet to think that Ned Bulmer is really anxious to marry into such a family, so blind, ignorant, conceited, and bitterly prejudiced. It can't be but that the granddaughter shares in all the foolish notions of the grandmother. She has been trained up in the same school. She thinks and feels precisely as the old woman does. That a son should desire to wed a woman who hates and despises the very race to which his father owes his origin!"

I must here advise the reader that this was said after Ned Bulmer had left us for the night, and when the Major and myself were lingering over our cigars, and a hot vessel of whiskey punch. Ned had disappeared purposely, in order that I might have every opportunity of subduing, if that were possible, the asperities and objections of the old man.

"You are mistaken, Major," said I, in reply, "in your opinion of Paula Bonneau. She shares in none of the prejudices of her grandmother, which ·she properly regards as most unhappy weaknesses. She is, herself, as liberal and intelligent a young woman as you will find in the country, noways arrogant or presumptuous, noways conceited or bigoted, and I believe quite as much an admirer of the English as of the Huguenot stock. Nay, the very favour with which she regards Ned seems to me quite conclusive on this point."

"Favour with which she regards Ned!" exclaimed the Major. "Why you don't mean to say it has got to that? You don't mean to tell me that they have already come to an understanding—that Ned has been so d——d precipitate as to propose, knowing my objections, and—"

Here he started to his feet, clapt his doubled fists into his ribs, and stood, arms akimbo, confronting me as if prepared for a regular engagement. I saw that I had been guilty of a lapse—had gone a step too far—and must recover.

" By no means," I answered with laborious coolness and delibe-ration, stirring my whiskey punch and blowing off the smoke. " That Paula favoured Ned is only a natural conclusion from her demeanour when they meet, and from the manner in which she speaks of him and of yourself. She *looks* as if she might love him, and speaks very kindly to and of him."

"Oh that is all, is it ! and well she may love him, and perfectly natural that she should desire him for a husband, for a better fel-low and a better looking fellow—though his own father I make bold to say it,—is nowhere to be found between the Santee and the Savannah. And she, too, is a clever girl enough, in her way, I do not doubt. I don't deny that she is pretty, and people every where say that she is amiable and intelligent ; but neverthe-less she is not the girl for Ned. She is too —— small, Dick ; that is one objection."

" Rather a recommendation, I should suppose, if, according to the proverb, a wife is, at best, a necessary evil."

"What ! of evils choose the least. But the smartness of the saying don't prove the philosophy to be good. Still, the objection of size might be overcome, if there were others not also insupera-ble. There's our family prejudice, Dick, against the race."

" Certainly—that objection could not be more impressively urged than by Madame Girardin, speaking of the English !"

" Confound her impudence. But there's no sense, Dick, in that. Her prejudices against the English, indeed ! What an old fool. Prejudices against the noblest people that God ever created, and whom he created to be the masters of the world,—the true successors to the Romans."

"That's just what she thinks of the French."

"Pshaw! the stubborn old dolt. Dont bring her up to me, Dick Cooper. The antipathy of the English to the French is based upon reason and experience. That of the French to the English is the natural result of fear and hatred, as the whipt dog dreads the scourge that has made him writhe and tremble. But, putting all this matter aside, Dick, there is still a better reason for my opposition to this passion of my son. The truth is,—and, for the present, this must be a secret between us,—I have already chosen a wife for Ned—"

"The d——l you have!" I exclaimed, starting up in my turn.

"No! But an angel I have; one of the most lovely creatures in the world—the very ideal of feminine beauty—a noble person, an exquisite skin, the sweetest and most brilliant eyes, lips that would make the mouth of a saint to water, and persuade an anchorite perpetually to sip,—and,—but enough. The woman upon whom I have set my eyes for Ned is, I hold, the perfection of woman!"

"And pray who is she?" I demanded, somewhat curious to know who could have inspired the Major with such raptures.

"Who! Can you doubt. Why, man, Beatrice Mazyck, to be sure!"

It was my turn to be confounded. Beatrice Mazyck! I wae staggered. You could have felled me with a feather. Beatrice Mazyck! My heart whirled about like the wheels of a locomotive. Beatrice Mazyck! What, the d——l, thought I, can the Fates be about? What do they design? What should put this notion into Major Bulmer's head, for my particular disquiet—perhaps defeat and disappointment. His wealth, his rank in the parish, his son's personal claims,—all rushed through my brain in

5

a moment, filling me with terror, and seeming conclusive of my own fate. I showed my consternation in my face.

"What's the matter with you, Dick,—you seem flurried ?"

"Nothing, I thank you, Major ; only I fancy this whiskey punch is a trifle too strong for my brain."

"Too strong ! Too weak rather ! Why, man, when I was of your age, we made no mouths at a pint of such liquor as that. A liquor which would laugh to shame all the nectar that the Greek gods stored away in their Olympian cellars. But the young men of this day are mere milksops. They have no heads— I may add no hearts also—such as they had when I was a boy. But what say you to Beatrice Mazyck ? Don't you approve of my choice ?"

The speech of the Major on the days of his youth, the strong heads and better hearts which they then enjoyed, afforded me time to recover from my consternation.. I felt that it was necessary for me to clothe myself in all my stoicism and meet the danger with becoming fortitude. I succeeded in the effort, and said—

"But, Major, how do you reconcile it to your *English* prejudices to think of Beatrice. She's as much French as Paula !"

"Hem !—yes !—not exactly. She has French blood in her veins, I grant you. But she is decidedly not French. The English predominates. Look at her figure. How thoroughly English. What a noble stature—what a fine bust—how well developed everywhere—then her face is Saxon—her skin fair, her eyes blue, her hair auburn—English all over !"

I laughed, in spite of my disquiet, at the ease with which prejudices may be overcome, when there's a will for it.

"You have reasoned yourself very happily into a new conviction, Major."

"Well, sir, and how should a man acquire new convictions, but through his reason. I claim to be a reasoning animal. Now, what objection have you to Beatrice Mazyck ?"

" For myself, none ; but for Ned—"

" Well, sir, for Ned ?   What objections do you make to her as a wife for Ned ?"

" First, then, I fancy he does not desire her."

" He's a fool, then, for his pains—but he will desire her, if his eyes can be reasonably opened. And you, my dear Dick, must assist me in becoming his occulist."

" Me, sir !—me, Major !"

" Yes, you ! Why not ! Why do you look so amazed at the suggestion ? You are the very man to do it ! You are Ned's friend— his confidant, his counsellor,—I may say his oracle.   Give me your assistance, and we shall soon contrive to persuade him that Beatrice is worth a hundred of his little French Paula."

" But, Major, suppose Beatrice should not altogether favour the arrangement.   What does she say about it ?"

" She will favour it, I'm sure.   Ned's not the fellow to sue for a lady's smiles in vain."

" Do you build solely on this.   Has Beatrice been sounded on the subject ?"

" Not yet, but she will be.   Her mother favours it."

" Ah !—well, sir ;—I am not sure that I can, for two reasons at least."

" Indeed !—well !—what are they."

" Firstly, as I said before, I'm pretty certain that Ned will never consent to substitute Paula for Beatrice.   He will never love Bea- trice.   Secondly, my dear Major, I want Beatrice for myself."

" The devil you do !" exclaimed the Major aghast, starting to his feet, and seizing me by the shoulder.

" Richard Cooper,—do you really mean it ?—are you in earn- est."

" As a prophet, sir."

" You love Beatrice Mazyck ?"

"From the bottom of my heart. I have loved her for two years."

"And she ?"—

"I have never approached her on the subject, sir."

"Then you are both uncommitted ?"

"Entirely—to each other."

"But has any thing served to encourage you, Dick ?"

"Nothing, sir, which a merely reasonable man would construe into a hope. I have sometimes fancied that she was not indifferent to me, and I have perhaps estimated her looks and words as significant of more than I could define or assert. But, beyond this, which may be wholly in my imagination, I have nothing upon which to found a hope."

"But, Dick, even did she favour you, are you in a condition to marry ? She is not rich, you know, and you—"

"Less so ! But that, Major, is a sufficient reason why we should both assert our independence. Poverty must not always stand upon ceremony. But, I frankly tell you, Major, were Beatrice willing, I should fearlessly venture upon matrimony with all its perils and expense !"

The old man strode the room with cloudy forehead and irregular motion. I, meanwhile, lighted a fresh cigar, and suffered my head to subside heavily between my shoulders, while I gazed into the fire sullenly, brooding upon newly aroused anxieties. After a while, the Major stopt in his walk, and confronted me :

"Dick, my boy, this is devilish unfortunate. You know my friendship for you, Dick,—my love for you, in fact,—for, in truth, I feel for you, next to my own boy, as if you were my own son. You rank next after him. I loved your father,—we were bosom friends, and stood beside each other in many a fight and frolic, even as you and Ned would, I am sure, stand up for each other. I would do a great deal for you, Dick, and should be glad to see you happy with the woman that you love ; but Dick, my heart is

set upon this marriage between Beatrice and Ned. I must do all
I can to promote it. I can think of no other woman for him, and,
in fact, have committed myself to her mother. But, Dick, it shall
be fair play between us. All shall be open and above board. You
will say nothing to Ned of my present objects, as I can now not
hope that you will say any thing in their favour; but I give you
notice, my boy, that I shall now go to work in earnest. What you
have so frankly told me compels me to anticipate as much as possible, and to urge, as rapidly as I can, an affair about which I had
meant to be deliberate. You, meanwhile, will do your best, and if
you can win the girl, in spite of all that I can do for Ned, then it
will prove that she is the proper person for you; and your success
shall be as satisfactory to me as to yourself. Nay, further, Dick, if
money can help you to a start in the world with Beatrice, you
shall have it. I can spare to you, without making bare myself,
and Ned, I'm sure, will do his part. Do your devoir, therefore, my
boy, with all your skill and spirit, as I am in honour bound to do
mine, and, as the old judges cried out in the courts of chivalry,
'God defend the right!' What's the old Norman French of it?
But, d—n the French of it! The English is good enough for my
purpose! Go ahead bravely,—there shall be no want of money,
Dick, for your progress, and we shall both equally acknowledge
that vital maxim to which our English ancestors owe, perhaps,
nine-tenths of their successes—'fair play!'"

The old man seized my hand, and shook it with a sternly sincere
emphasis. I answered the grasp with like fervour, but I could say
nothing. I was very deeply touched with his nobleness and
generosity. Certainly, with all his prejudices, the Major is one of
the most noble specimens of modern manhood.

"And now, Dick," said he, "to bed. Finish your punch, and
we'll be off. We must rise by daylight for the hunt to-morrow.
'This day a deer must die!'"

And he went off humming the ballad.

5*

CHAPTER VII.

" Bucks have at ye all.*"—Old Song.*

At dawn the horns were sounding, and the beagles yelling all
around the premises.   Major Bulmer had a noble pack of hounds,
thirty in number.   This was one of his weaknesses—he was ambitious of keeping up the old practice of his grandfather,—to say
nothing of his English authorities,—although circumstances had
quite changed.   Ours are no longer the vast forests that they were
prior to '76.   The swamps are no longer inaccessible, and the
population, greatly increased, give the deer no respite.   Accordingly, they are terribly thinned off, and it is quite an event when an
overseer or driver can say to the planter, "there's an old buck
about,"—or, "there's tracks of deer in the peafield."   What a
blowing of horns follows such an annunciation !   What a chorus
of dogs !   What a mustering of Mantons and full-bloods.   There
is no slumbering thence, for the household, till we have "got the
meat !"   "This day a deer must die !" cried Ned Bulmer, booming
into my room before the sun had fairly rubbed his eyes for a rising,
echoing the burthen which had sounded last in my ears, when I
lay down to sleep.   I was upon my feet in the twinkling of an eye,
for, though a bookworm of late, and a city lawyer, I had been once
a famous fellow for the chase, was a free rider, a good shot, and
altogether a good deal of a hunter.   It had been a passion with
me once, but—what has poverty to do with passion !   Mine seemed bent equally to interfere with me in my pursuit of *deer* and
dear.   I thought of Beatrice, and the last night's conversation
with the Major, the moment I opened my eyes ; and I confess I
looked at Ned Bulmer, born to fortune and having it forced upon
him, as it were, with a momentary feeling of envy.   Thanks to
the Virgin, I soon dismissed the despicable feeling with scorn.

The frank, noble features of my friend, in which every secret feeling of his soul was declared, soon set mine to rights; and I said to myself—"Be it so! At all events, Beatrice, whether you get Ned Bulmer or myself, you will be equally fortunate in the possession of one of the best fellows in the world." It might have made Ned blush had I repeated this compliment in his ears, so I prudently kept it to myself, satisfied that there was no sort of necessity for my own blushes.

Adonization is not a difficult process with the hunter, when the dogs are at the overture. I had soon made my toilet. Our guns had been put in order the night before. By candlelight we now loaded them. Then followed a bowl of coffee all round, and the horn of the old Major sounded for the start. We were soon off at an easy pace, having about two miles to ride before we reached the stands. These were well known places, gaps and openings, by certain favourite runs of water, or crossing places from wood to wood. The simple secret of a hunter's stand, is to find out the avenues which the deer lays out for himself. All animals are creatures of habit, and, unless under good and sufficient reasons, the herd usually adheres to its ordinary pathways. But these, in a very large tract of forest, are apt to be numerous, and to require a large number of hunters. Our present *drives*, however, were small ones, and soon covered. There were no hunters in our present party, but the Major, Ned, myself, and the overseer, a sprightly and intelligent young fellow named Benbow. In all probability the name was that originally of an old English archer, and was corrupted and contracted from Jack, or Dick, Bend the Bow, to its present narrow and unimpressive limits of two syllables short. We had all of us *stanas*, each watching his avenue. Sam, the negro *driver*, put in with the dogs, some three quarters of a mile above us, eating his way through all the denser coppices of a thick mixed wood of scrubby oak and pine, having a close underbrush, and sundry good feeding places, from which the fire was carefully kept

out. But I must not linger on these details. Every body nearly
knows what is the usual deer hunting among the gentry of the
South.   There is little about it that is complicated ; its success de-
pending upon a knowledge of the drives, the stands, a cool head,
quick eye, sure shot, and occasionally a keen spur to the flanks of
a smoking courser; for it is no small accomplishment to know
how to head a deer, and to succeed, by a swift circuit, in doing it.
Let it suffice that we had not long to wait.   The dogs soon gave
tongue—the cries thickened—anon I heard a shot from the Major,
who was just above me, and a few moments after, head forward,
tail up, streaking away for *dear* (deer) life, at about eighty yards
to the left, I got a glimpse of the victim, a buck in full feather, i. e.
with a noble pair of branches.   It was instinct purely—a word
and a blow, and the blow first.   I popt away at him, and saw him
describe a short turn, setting his head in the opposite direction.   I
concluded he had got it, but could not afford a second glance, as I
caught sight of a couple of does following steadily his course,
though a little nearer to me than he had been when I first shot,
and almost in the same line.   I had another barrel, and bestowed
it successfully.   Down dropt one of the brown beauties, and I
sounded.   The dogs, meanwhile, began to glimmer, on full foot,
through the leaves.   My horse was hitched twenty feet behind
me.   It took but a minute to unhitch and cross him, and I pushed
for my victims.   In a few moments the Major came dashing up,
like a fiery boy of eighteen, shouting out—

   " Well, Dick, what's the sport.   I fancy you've wasted lead, for
I gave it to the old buck that passed you, and I never miss.   But
you emptied both barrels."

   " Here's one of my birds," I answered, pointing to the doe, from
which we drove off the dogs, setting them on the track of the
old buck, who had shed a gill of the purple fluid within fifteen
steps of the place where the dead doe lay.

"Do you see that, Major," I said, pointing to the crimson drop-
lets still warm upon the yellow leaves of autumn.

"Yes," said he, "a mortal hit! frothy; from the lungs! Push
on, Benbow, or the dogs will tear the meat. But I am sure that
he carries my lead also. I never missed him, Dick; couldn't do
such a thing at my time of life."

"Well, sir, we'll see. I can tell you, when the buck was near-
ing me, he didn't show signs of hurt! There may have been
two."

"No! only one! I've surely hit him. I'll stake a cool hundred on it."

And we rode forward, Ned joining us meanwhile. The deer had
left him entirely to the right. He had seen nothing of either.
We soon found the old buck, just dead. The shot that killed him
was mine, given directly behind the right fore-quarter, as he pushed
obliquely from me. But the exulting Major discovered other
button holes in the jacket of the beast, to which he laid confident
claim. It was not a matter which could be proved, so, accordingly, it was not exactly the matter to be discussed. We all readily
recognized the claim of the old man to have certainly made his
mark, if he had not exactly made his meat. It was admitted,
however, to be quite a feather in my cap, that, fresh from the
dingy chambers of the law, and the ponderous volumes of the frosty
wigs, I should still have had my nerves and senses in such good
training for the sports of the field.

"The law has not spoiled you for a gentleman and a hunter yet,"
quoth the Major encouragingly. "And that is saying something;
for many's the pretty fellow whom I've known it ruin for all proper purposes."

Our hunt was over by two o'clock, and our game bagged.
When we reached "the Barony," we found it full of guests. Se-
veral fine spirited fellows were there, the Porchers, Ravenels,
Cordes, and others, as guests to dinner; and they were all full-

mouthed in their reproaches that they had not been summoned to the hunt. We made up a party for another day, and adjourned to dinner. Night found us still at the table, for the Major's wines had a proverbial smack of ancient magic. They were such as Mephistophiles himself could scarcely have made to spout out from the best timber in the Black Forest. Whist that night, and whiskey punch in the library, kept us busy till twelve, when, by common consent, we called in Morpheus to light us to our chambers.

CHAPTER VIII.

INTRIGUE AND LOVE—SHUFFLING THE CARDS.

DAYS and nights pass with singular rapidity at a southern plantation. Visitor succeeds to visitor, dinner to dinner, and every day is employed, during the winter holidays at least in preparing for the recreation of its successor. What, with old acquaintances to be seen, and the promotion of Ned's *affair*, I was incessantly employed. Besides, the Major's circle was perpetually full ; and I was frequently detained at "the Barony" engaged in seeing visitors, when both Ned and myself desired to be abroad. The day after the hunt, after making a circuit and two or three calls, we found ourselves, at one o'clock, once more at the Girardin estate, where I left my friend, to make another visit to the stately Madame Agnes-Theresa. Ned, meanwhile, wandered off to the grove between the two places, an anxious waiter upon that friendly Providence which is supposed generally to take the affairs of love in hand. Talk of true love's course not running smoothly ! The fact is, that, after certain consideration and a certain experience, I am assured that few true lovers ever have much reason to complain. Love has an instinct in discovering its proper mate, and suppose there are obstacles? These really heighten the charm of pursuit, and increase the luxuries of conquest. Stolen fruit is proverbially the sweetest, and stolen kisses are such as the lips never quite lose the taste of. The first kiss lingers in memory, softening the heart to fondness, even after the time has passed when any kiss affords a pleasure; and, to man or woman, I suspect, he or she who has first taught us the subtle and delicious joy of that first kiss, is remembered with a sense of gratitude, even when there is no warmer emotion inspired by the same person. To Ned and the lovely Paula, I am persuaded that the stolen interviews which I succeeded in procuring them, will be among their dearest recollections in after days. Not that dear little Paula ever crept away to that grove without fear and misgiving. She wasn't sure that it was right to do so; but that did not lessen the pleasure of the thing. Again and again they met, and the child murmured, and sighed, and wept, and was made happy through all her fears and tears. And Ned was happy too, though he always came back growling from the interview. It was always so short. Paula was always in such a hurry to break away! Certainly, make them as happy as you please, you cannot easily make young lovers contented. He who steals the fruit, is always sorry to leave the tree behind him. Enough, that on this, as on the preceding evening, I was quite successful in beguiling the grandmother with long discourse, thus affording Paula an opportunity to steal away and meet her lover. Do not be angry with her, ye prudes who have survived these sympathies of seventeen. You have done likewise, every one of you, in turn, or, if you have not, the merit of forbearance was none of yours. You would have done so, loving with the innocent fondness of Paula, and with such a manly and noble swain as Ned Bulmer to persuade you to the groves. Well, they met, and mingled sighs and promises of fidelity; but in vain did Ned entreat his beauty to a clandestine marriage. Believing that he should never conquer the prejudices of his father, or subdue the stubborn pride of Madame Bonneau, Ned was thus desperate in his projects. But sweet little Paula was firm on this subject.

"I will never love any but you, Edward—never marry any but you—but cannot consent to a secret marriage."

"But they will always oppose us, Paula!" said the lover, vehemently.

"Then I must die!" murmured the maiden, with her head drooping on his bosom. And then he protested that she should not die; that he would sooner die himself; nay, kill a great many other people, not omitting the obstinate grandmother, and the cruel father, and many other desperate things; all of which dear little Paula begged him not to do, "for her sake,"—and for her sake only, he magnanimously consented to forbear these bloody performances. But why linger on the child prattle of young lovers—so sweet but so simple; so ridiculous, to our thoughts, as we grow older; yet so precious and full of meaning when we took part in it, and in which the heart never becomes quite too old to partake, when ever the opportunity and the object are afforded it. At last they separated, with the sweet kiss, and the assuring promise of fidelity; both believing implicitly as if specially guaranteed by heaven. Paula reappeared, and relieved me of my friendly drudgeries with grandmamma, suffering the same rebuke, as before, for her disappearance. The next day, the Major, Ned and myself, rode over to Mrs. Mazyck's, about four miles distant, to make our obeisance. Our readers know what are the objects of the 'Baron.' Ned, already, I fancy, suspected the designs of the father, from the pains he took to discourage them. But, supposing *me* ignorant of these designs, and knowing my passion for Beatrice, he was scrupulously careful to avoid the subject. His deportment, when we met the ladies, gave me no occasion for jealousy. We spent an hour with them, and the Major, devoting himself to the mother, left the field to us wholly, so far as the young lady was concerned. Ned, in a degree following his father's example, now left the field to me, and strolled off from the parlour into the library, giving me sufficient opportunity to play what card I pleased in the game. When the Major and Mrs. Mazyck returned from the garden, whither they had gone to trace the progress of certain rare seedlings in the hot-house, they found Beatrice and myself, alone together.

The mother looked grave, and the Major impatiently asked after his son. Of course, neither of us knew where he was.— When he was hunted up, we found him stretched, at length, on the sofa in the library, enveloped in the most downy embraces of sleep. The Major roused him with a fierce shake of the shoulder, and looked at him with the scowl of a thunderstorm. Ned took the whole affair very quietly ; and we mounted our horses a few moments after. When fairly off, and out of the gates, the old man blazed out with his volcanic matter.

"A d—d pretty puppy you are, sir, to go to sleep when visiting a lady ! Do you not know, sir, how much I respect Mrs. Mazyck, sir ?"

"Well, sir, so do I, but you took her off yourself. You did'nt leave me to entertain her. I had reason to be jealous, sir, of your attentions."

"Jealous ! The d—l ! But I left you and Dick to entertain the young lady, sir."

"And I assure you, father, that Dick is perfectly adequate to the task alone. I felt that I should be *de trop*."

" *De*—what ! why the devil will you abuse my ears with that atrocious lingo ? Leave it off, sir, if you please; in my hearing, at least. I repeat, sir, you treated Miss Beatrice with marked disrespect."

"You are quite mistaken, sir. I treated her with marked consideration. Ask the question of herself, and she will tell you that she greatly appreciates the attentions which I paid her. Be

6

assured, she has no sort of cause for, or feeling of, disappointment."

" Blockhead! you know not the mischief you do by this conduct."

" Indeed, sir! Pray how? Anything serious?"

" Puppy!" exclaimed the complimentary sire, looking at me with a glance, as if to say—" what a beautiful game of mine does the fellow strive to spoil,"—but he forbore his speech, and only used his spurs; driving them into his horse's flanks, and setting off at a canter that soon left us far behind him.

" Let him go, Dick, while we quietly jog on, and do the civil thing to one another. Dad is by no means in a complimentary mood to-day. The truth is, he is for making up a match between Beatrice Mazyck and myself, but that match won't burn, *mon ami*. I see what he's after, and must prepare for the explosion. It will blow out, and blow over, before many days."

When we got to " the Barony," the Major was no where to be seen. He had retired to his chamber to soothe his anger by a temporary resort to solitude.

" But," says Ned, " solitude was never a favourite passion with him; and we shall have him down upon us directly. Meanwhile, let us have some wine."

We had just filled our glasses when the old man, sure enough, made his appearance. He was cloudy, but no longer savage. He treated me with rather marked civilities, which I did not exactly like; but for Ned he had very few words. Dinner brought him soothing; and that night, when Ned left us together, as he thought it his policy to do, the Major recovered his wonted kindness and frankness, over a hot glass of whiskey toddy.

" That boy put me out to-day, Dick, as he gave you all the chances. Of course you made the best use of them. I confess it makes me angry. His reluctance spoils a favourite plan. I don't despair of him yet, and the game will need to be played frequently, before it finishes. You have made a point in it; and I could almost say that I am glad, for your sake, that you have. Certainly, Dick, though you may see me ruffled with that cub of mine, in this matter, don't suppose that I shall ever feel any unkindness towards you. Go ahead, as I said before. There shall be 'fair play' between us."

Such was the purport of our chat that night, the Major getting over his moody humour before he had entirely got through his toddy. And so, day and night went by in rapid succession; society daily; the hunt, the dinner, the visitor, and, I confess, the nightly potation, sometimes with larger liberties than are usually accorded by the just Temperance standards. Another morning call upon Madame Girardin, which she received only as my own proper tribute to herself—proof of my good taste and good sense, and her acknowledged rights—and then came a formal invitation to the widow Mazyck's on a certain evening, by which we knew that a grand party was intended. Ned smiled, as the billets were handed in by the waiter.

"Miching malico!" quoth he. "The fight thickens, Dick.— It will soon become highly interesting. Well; we shall go of course. I have a faith in parties, and some taste for them. I love dancing, and I shall find Paula there, who is an angel on the wing on such occasions. I mean to be quite attentive this time, so that Dad shall have no reason to complain. Whether I shall altogether please him by the sort of person I shall choose, on whom to bestow my attentions, is a question which he may resolve for my benefit, or his own, hereafter."

When, an hour after, in the library with the Major, he showed me his invitation, and said—

"Well, Dick, here are the chances for both of us. I shall have a talk with Ned, and try to spirit him on to his duty. He can't altogether neglect the lady; and when he sees Beatrice in contrast with his little Frenchified puppet, I am in hopes that he will see her somewhat with your eyes. At all events, Dick, if we are to be beaten by you in the game, it will be some consolation to me that you are the successful player. But I shall do my best to thwart you, my boy, if I can, so long as it is possible to do any thing for Ned. But all in love, Dick, be assured; nothing in malice!"

And with a warm and friendly gripe of the hand, we separated for the night.

CHAPTER IX.

"Let me help you to a wife, sir."
"Help yourself, *sir*."—*Old Play.*

LET us suppose the time to have elapsed, and the night to have arrived for the party at Mrs. Mazyck's. We set out an hour by sun for her place, the Major and Ned taking the buggy of the latter, while I accompanied Miss Bulmer, the maiden sister of the former. The Major contrived this arrangement the better to inform his companion, along the way, touching his wishes, and the particular deportment which he expected of the latter, when he had reached the scene of action. He had, during the day, been showing me, in part, what he meant to say to Ned; painting Beatrice Mazyck to me in the most glowing colours, and evidently memorizing, for future use, certain wonderfully flowery phrases, which he had recalled from his early reading of such poets as had been popular in his day. He was as impatient for the hour of starting as myself, and we set off, all of us, under some excitement; Ned anticipating all that he should hear; the Major anxious to be delivered of his eloquence; Miss Bulmer thinking of large revenues of parish chit chat; and I, shall I confess it, eager for the meeting with one whom I yet approached with fear and trembling, no less than love!

Ned and his father followed us, the latter having delayed his movements purposely to suffer the carriage to go ahead. To my friend, subsequently, I owed a full account of the conversation.

'The Governor,' said he, 'began with a long exordium, intending to show me that he had lived solely for my happiness and not for his own. To hear him, one would suppose, that, but for the well-beloved son, he would have been better pleased to lie down in the grave in peace. Yet no man loves a good dinner more sincerely, or smacks his lips after a glass of madeira with a more infinite sense of prevailing thirst. To see me happy and successful—to see me well married, in brief, before he died—was to him the only remaining desire of his life. He asked me almost sternly, if I did not believe the marriage state, the natural and proper state of man? I told him—as I really thought—'and of woman too.' 'No jests, Ned,' said he, 'the subject is a very serious one.' 'Even gloomy I should say, sir, judging from your visage and tones at this moment. Really, sir, if you look so wretched on the subject, I shall be frightened forever from its consideration.' 'Pshaw! you are a fool,' said he, 'it is so far serious as the subject of human happiness is the serious question of human life.' 'Don't agree with you!' said I. 'I don't see that we've any need to bother our brains with such a subject. The business of mortal life is *not* happiness, if it be true that our business is the establishing of a right to happiness hereafter. I suppose it is the proper question for mule, horse, cow or dog, which have nothing but the present to take care of; but is clearly not the one for us.' 'And what is the question for us, Mr. Philosopher?' 'Clearly *duty!*' 'Precisely,' quoth the Governor, 'and is it not your duty, at a certain time in life, to get yourself a wife?' 'Tolerable rhyme enough,' said I, 'no matter what may be the value of the philosophy.' 'Don't vex me, Ned,' said he, 'but speak seriously.

6*

Don't you conceive it to be your duty, now that you are twenty-one, or near it, to be looking about you for a help-meet?' 'Or a help-eat meat—which I take to be the more appropriate phrase usually.' 'You are enough, sir, to vex Saint Francis? Can't you answer a straight question?' 'How can that be a straight question which concerns a *rib?*' 'What a vile attempt at wit! A punster is always a puppy!' 'And if so a physician!' 'Why, sir?' 'He deals in *bark!*' 'Pshaw, Ned! Have done with that, and answer me like a man of sense. I tell you that I am very serious. I contend that you ought to be thinking of a wife.' 'Well, sir, I have given you to understand that I *have* been thinking of one.' 'What! that little Bonneau! But that's out of the question, I tell you. I will never consent to any such folly. Let me choose a wife for you?' 'Really, sir, that's almost as reasonable a demand as if I had claimed the right before I was born to have chosen my own mother. I protest, sir, I hold it abominable that, not content with choosing for yourself, you should also assert the privilege of selecting for me the mother of my children. Don't you think, sir, that you might just as reasonably make it a requisition in your will, that your grand-children, male or female, shall only marry persons of a certain figure—measured proportions, defined temperaments, colour of hair, and skin, form of chin and mouth—all accurately described?' 'And it would be a devilish sight better for the race, could the thing be done. We should then have fewer puppies and dolls to destroy the breed in noble families. But to the point. I tell you, sir, you must think no more of this little Frenchwoman.' 'Frenchwoman, sir! Why Paula Bonneau is as much an American and a South Carolinian as yourself.' 'The Americans are not a race, sir. As for the South Carolinians, sir, I doubt if, just at this moment, we ought to speak of them at all. I am not satisfied that the subject affords us any cause of satisfaction. We are not in a condition for boasting, sir, any longer. All of our great men have gone; and

the labours of our little men, to put on the strut of greatness, is
that froggish emulation of oxlike developement which the old fable
finds for our benefit. Indeed, the condition of our country is one
of the reasons why I am so anxious that you should marry wisely.
There is nothing so important as that you should get a woman,
sir, a *real* woman, and not a child—not a chit—as the mother of
my grand-children. I want the name of Bulmer, sir, transmitted
through a race fearless in spirit, generous in impulse, active in
thought, and noble in figure. Sir, it is impossible that such nopes
can be realized in wiving with such an insignificant little thing—'
'Stop, sir,' said I, 'go no farther. I will listen to you reverently
enough so long as you forbear what is offensive to Paula Bonneau!' The old man muttered something savagely between his
closed teeth; then, impatiently—' Well, sir, I will endeavour not
to tread upon your corns, since you are so monstrous sensitive
about them. I will say nothing in disparagement of the one,
while urging the claims of the other lady. Ned, my son, you do
not doubt that I love you; that I think for you, strive for you,
and that my chief solicitude in life is that you may be settled in
such a way, before I leave it, as will be most likely to ensure your
happiness.' The Governor was evidently disposed to try the pathetic on me. 'But, sir, you are hardly likely to do this, if you
deny me the right of thinking for myself. On a matter of this
sort, sir, a young man is more apt to be tenacious of his rights,
than upon any other subject. I am perfectly persuaded that you
should choose a horse for me, sir. I know you have an excellent
eye to horses, can trace blood and determine pedigree to a fraction,
and know the good points of draught or saddle horses at the
glance of an eye. I am not unwilling to believe, sir, that your
judgment is equally infallible in hounds and pointers. I've observed *that*, sir, a hundred times. In the matter of dogs and
horses, sir, I would leave everything to your judgment; but really, sir, regarding a woman, or a wife, by standards wholly differ-

ent, I confess, if a wife is to be chosen, I should prefer pleasing
my own eye to pleasing yours.   I assure you, sir, that if it were
your present purpose to choose one for yourself, I should not interfere with your judgment in the slightest degree.'   'You are
enough to irritate a Saint, Ned Bulmer, and I have half a mind
to take you at your word, marry again, and cut you off without
a shilling.   But I know you for a teazing puppy, and you shan't
ruffle me.   If I did not know that you conceal a good heart and
a noble nature under this garment of levity—did I not know that
you have a proper veneration for me as your father, sir, I should
tumble you headlong out of the buggy.   You shall hear me nevertheless.   I want you to marry.   I have said so.   You wish to
marry.'   'I have said it.'   'But not the right woman.   Now, I
have chosen the right woman for you; I have opened a negocia-
tion with Mrs. Mazyck for her daughter, Beatrice, for you!'   'What,
sir, have you two wicked old people devoted us as a burnt offer-
ing, two innocent lambs to the sacrifice, without so much as saying a word to either of us on the subject.'   'I am saying it to
you now.'   'But after you have managed every thing.   And
here you would drag us away, with flowers perhaps about our
brows, and chain us, a pair of consecrated victims at the altar of
your pride and avarice.   Shame on you, papa, and shame on you,
mamma, for these cruel doings.'   The mock heroic was too much
for the old Major's philosophy.   But his rage strove with the ludicrous in his fancy.   He swore and laughed in the same breath.

'Papa,' I continued, 'you're going to make me behave cruelly.
Whenever you say or do a foolish, or wicked, or cruel thing, I'll
whip the horse.   You'll see!   I can't lay the whip on you, but
I'll show my sense of what you deserve, by scoring the flanks of
White Raven!   I will!   I owe him more than twenty cuts already.'   And, saying these words, I popped the lash over the
quarter of the horse twice or thrice, before he could arrest my
hand.   'Why, are you mad?' said he, seizing the whip, or making

an effort to do so. 'No, sir, not mad, but highly indignant. Somebody wants a sound whipping, and I must bestow it on something.' 'Well,' said he, with more composure than I expected, 'I fancy your next proceeding will be to try your whip on my shoulders.' 'Oh! no, sir! never; though, if you were seriously to ask me the question, I should say, that if grand-papa were still living, I should be apt to request him to subject you to some of the ancient forms of mortification and flagellation.' 'Ned,' said he, 'my dear son, let me entreat you to give me your serious attention. Believe me, I was never more serious in my life. I wish you to look upon Beatrice Mazyck with the eyes of a lover, and pay all proper court to her in that capacity. I have spoken with her mother. She favours the match, and I am therefore really and earnestly committed to her. Now, my son, do not forget what you owe to the wishes of your father. It is probable that Mrs. Mazyck has spoken with Beatrice, even as I have spoken with you, and, in all probability, the young lady will expect your attentions, as I know her mother will. Do not trifle with her feelings, my son, and I pray you respect mine.' He said a great deal more, when, becoming seriously vexed, I kept still while he exhausted himself. Finding I still kept silence, he asked— 'Well, Ned, what do you say?' 'What can I say, sir? It seems to me that I am the person for whom a wife is wanted. I choose one woman, and you another. I don't see, sir, how we are to reconcile our differences in taste.' 'But, Ned, the woman of whom you speak is by no means suitable.' 'That, sir, seems a question proper only to myself to determine. The whole question resolves itself to this. Either I am under a despotism, or I am not. You would not undertake, sir, to force me to eat cabbage at your table whether I wanted it or not. Yet, sir, it would be quite an innocent tyranny to force me to eat cabbage against my will, compared to that of compelling me to take a wife against my will!' 'Do you mean to compare Beatrice Mazyck to a cabbage?' 'Heaven for-

bid, sir, that I should do any thing so irreverent or ungallant.—
But I do not take to Beatrice, nor I suspect, she to me.' 'But
try her, at least. 'Why, sir, when I don't want her, and when,
in all probability, she is as little desirous of me?' 'For my sake,
Ned, do the courteous thing, and we know not but you will come
to relish one another.' 'I will do anything in reason for your
sake, father, but this is not reasonable; and your intriguing nego-
ciations with the mother of the one lady may do equal wrong to
her and to myself, and lead to confusion, if not misery, all round.'
'It's too late now, Ned; I am commited—think of that! I am
committed! My honour is committed. Your father's honour.'
'You have no doubt erred, sir, but your committal is one for
which reason, common sense, human nature, will all furnish you
in a moment, a reasonable apology to any reasoning and intelligent mother. But, that *you* are committtted, does not seem to me
to involve any necessity why you should commit me also. This
philosophy is that of the old fox, who went once too often to the
rat-trap, and then discoursed to his brethren of the indecency of
wearing tails. You have never found me a wilful or disobedient
son, my father; why force me now, by a tyranny which society
no longer tolerates—which has become wholly traditional with
the tales of Blue Beard and other Barons—not of Carolina—to
show that insubordination which I never exhibited before.' 'Tyranny! You call me a tyrant, Ned?' 'According to my notions, if you urge this matter, you will be. People think differ-
ently about tyranny and tyrants. One man, doing a merciless
act, will fancy no cruelty in the performance if he smile upon the
victim, and use the gentlest language, while he goads him to extremity. Your Jack Ketch is a notorious humanitarian—a fellow
of most benevolent stomach, who will beg your forgiveness and
your prayers, while adjusting the knot in 'gingerly fashion' under your left lug. I've no doubt you'd carry me to the altar,—
which, unless I am suffered to choose my own wife, I'd as lief

should be the halter—with the most parental tenderness. You'd try to reconcile me to the rope by giving me a glorious wedding-supper, and the next morning, I should receive deeds conveying to me your best plantation and a hundred negroes.' 'Well, sir?' 'Well, sir, I say, rather than marry the wife of another man's choosing, I'd fling deed, and estate, and negroes into the fire, and plough my own road to fortune in the worst sand lands of the country. You have not the fortune, sir, even if you gave me all that you have and could bestow, that can reconcile me to the bitter physic you require me to take as the condition by which it is obtained.' With that I scored the horse, saying as I did so— 'But here we are, sir, at Bonneau Place; I suppose it will be proper only to say no more, just now, on the subject.' He put his hand on my arm—'My dear Ned, for my sake, do the civil thing by Miss Mazyck. Pay her every attention, dance with her, see her to supper, and—' 'Enough, my dear father, enough! I shall certainly not do anything to forfeit the character of a gentleman. But, be sure, I shall not do any thing which shall lead her to suppose that I am ambitious of the attitude of a lover.' The old man threw himself back in the buggy in a desponding attitude, muttering something which I did not make out, and in the next moment we dashed into the court among a dozen other vehicles.

CHAPTER X.

HOW WE DANCED, AND SUPPED, AND SO—FORTH!

The Mazyck establishment was on an extensive scale. It was its ancient baronial features that had insensibly impressed the imagination of Major Bulmer. The house was a vast one for our country—a massive mansion of brick, opening upon a grand passage way, or hall in the centre, from which you diverged into double rooms on either hand. These were of larger size than usual in our country seats. These also had wings, consisting each of a single room over the basement, and lower by one story than the main building. One of these, devoted to the library, was thrown open on the present occasion. The other was a sort of state chamber, meant for guests of distinction, special favourites, or for newly married couples. The floors were magnificently carpeted, and the rooms elegantly furnished. They were already beginning to fill on our arrival; the custom of the country differing from that of the city in requiring the guests to come early, however late they may be persuaded to stay. Very soon the bustle of first arrivals was at an end: only now and then, an occasional annunciation betokened some visitor who still held to the city rule of late arrivals, or who, most probably, was ambitious of an innovation upon country habits. A vulgar self-esteem always comes late to church or into society, if only with the view of making a sensation. At eight o'clock tea was served, with the usual accompaniments of cake and cracker. Quite a creditable display of silver plate was justified by this service, and the green beverage sent up such savoury odours of the Land of Flowers, as would have stirred even the obtuse olfactories of Sam Johnson. Suppose the company all arranged, rather formally around the parlour, with glimpses of groups of young persons especially in the library, all busy in the kindred occupations of tea and talk, fifty cups smoking and as many tongues making music, and we may now look round the circle, and take in its several aspects. Tall, stately, the form and features of my antique friend, Madame Agnes-Theresa, rise, supreme over all presences, in erect dignity, starched cap and handkerchief, scant locks of pepper and salt, and sharp eyes that suffer no evasion or escape. I approach, I bend before her, I crave to be blessed with her smiles, and she accords them. But where is pretty Paula? In the library with the young people. Ah! and Ned Bulmer is already hovering about her, as the moth about the flame. The Major sees him not as yet, being exceedingly earnest in his attentions to Mrs. Mazyck. The veteran is displaying the graces of manner which constituted the ton thirty-five or forty years ago. Then it was all elaborate courtesies—a bow was a thing of ceremonial—the right toe had its given route prescribed in one direction, the left in another—off at right angles; the arms were spread abroad in a waving course, the hands inclining to the knees—which, as the back was bent like a bow at the stretch, enabled them almost to clasp them.— The head slightly thrown back, the chin peering out, an ineffable smile upon the lips, and a profound admiration expressed in the eyes, and you have the attitude, air and manner of the ancient beau ready to do battle and die in your behalf. That careless, effortless, informal manner, which marked the *insouciant* character of our day, was, with the excellent Major, only a dreadful proof of the degeneracy of the race.

"A fellow now-a-days," quoth he, "enters a room, as if he sees nobody or cares for nobody; as if he owned pretty much all that he sees; he slides, or rather saunters in with the listless air of a man picking his teeth after dinner—anon, he catches a glance of somebody whom he condescends to know; and it is—'Ah, Miss Eveline, or Isabella, or Maria, or Teresa, how d'ye—glad to see you looking so—ah!—well! and how's your excellent mamma? Hope the dear old lady keeps her own. Good for fifty years yet; and how long have you been from town? Very dull here; don't ye think so?—ah-h-h!' yawning as if he had toiled all day and caught no fish. Talk of such fellows, indeed. They seem to be made out of nothing but wire and whale-bone, with a pair of butterfly wings which they can't fly with, and such a voice, like that of an infant frog with rather a bad cold for such a juvenile. Sad degeneracy! Very different, Mrs. Mazyck, from the men of *our* day.'

7

Talking with Beatrice Mazyck, three removes from him, I contrived to hear every syllable, and whispered her at the moment. He turned just then, and detected the movement. He joined us in a second, and with a profound bow to the lady, and a smile of kindness to me, he said—

" I see you heard me, my dear Miss Beatrice, by the laughing smile upon your countenance. I do not know whether you agree with me, or can agree with me, since you have no opportunity of knowing the manners of a day long before your own."

" Unless," quickly and archly answered the lady, " unless from the excellent occasional example which has been preserved to the present time, and from which we are compelled to feel that there is more truth in your report, than we are willing to acknowledge. What say you, Mr. Cooper ?"

" Nay, do not ask him," said the Major, " for, of a truth, to do him justice, he is one of the few exceptions which the present day offers to the uniform degeneracy of its young men. Dick Cooper is a favourite of mine, and particularly so from his freedom from all affectations. He does'nt affect ease, by a most laborious suppression of dignity and manhood—to say nothing of grace."

This was very handsome of the Major, and I felt that I ought to blush if I did not, but I replied without seeming to notice the compliment.

" I am inclined to think, Major, that the two periods simply occupied extremes, neither significant of sincerity. In fact, conventional life seems of its own nature to forbid sincerity, inasmuch as it denies earnestness. Now, the school which you so admirably represent, Major, appears to me to have sought for *finish* at every sacrifice ; and to have aimed at the application of court manners on reception days to the business of ordinary social life. I confess, for my own part, though I try to be as profound in my courtesies as possible, I can not well persuade myself to emulate or imitate, even if that were possible, the elaborate bow with which you bent before Mrs. Mazyck, or even that still more elaborate, if less courteous obeisance which you made when passing Mrs. Bonneau. There is no doubt that the contrast which you speak of is indicative of moral changes of a serious character in the race. As the court usher of Louis XV. detected the approaching revolution in the ribands in the shoes of the courtier noble, in place of the golden buckle, so does the substitution of the jaunty, indifferent manner of the modern gentleman betray the dislike to form, restraint, and all authority—in a word, that utter decline of reverence—which promises to be the great virtue in the eyes of ultrademocracy, the maxim of which is—'The world's mine oyster.' The eye of our times takes in all things that it sees, and at once acquires a right therein; and even the smiles of beauty, are things of course, which to behold is necessarily to command.—Whether we do not lose by this confidence in ourselves,—for this is the true signification of it all,—is a question which I do not propose to argue. I am of the opinion, my dear Major, that a compromise might well be made between the manners of your day and ours—when ease of manner might be regulated and restrained by a courtly grace, and a gentle solicitude, and when dignity might be held back from the embraces of formality."

"Ah! Dick, that would be quite a clever essay, and full of suggestiveness, but for that atrocious word 'compromise.' The compromises of modern democracy are the death of our securities, and democracy is but that 'universal wolf,' as described by Shakspeare,

> " Which makes perforce an universal prey,
> And last, eats up itself."

You remember the passage; and that which follows is the clue to the whole evil—

> " This chaos when *Degree* is suffocate,
> Follows the choking."

The Major had got upon a favourith text, and was not soon

suffocate himself. It is not possible for me to follow him, nor is it desirable that I should. He gave me at the close a sly look, saying—

"I must go see after Ned. Ah! Dick, if he only had the good taste which you have, and knew as well how to lead out trumps in a game like ours."

This was all said in a whisper. He disappeared leaving me still to play the cards in my possession. What need I speak of the game? Suffice it that I played, not presumptuously, and yet I trust manfully. At all events, I secured the hand of Beatrice Mazyck—for the first cotillion.

Tea disappeared, an interregnum followed, in which the buz was universal, and mostly unintelligible except to a few who contrived, like myself, to monopolize a corner and a companion. Soon, there was a slight bustle, and a fair-haired and fair-cheeked girl, a Miss Starke, from one of the middle districts, was conducted to the piano, which she approached with hesitating steps; but the hesitancy ceased when her fingers began to commerce with the keys. She executed the Moses in Egypt of Rossini, with a nice appreciation, and secured a very tolerable hearing from the audience; a song followed from a Miss Walter, of some one of the parishes; and then a lively overture from the violin in the passage-way silenced the piano for the rest of the night, signalizing a general and very animating bustle. There were two violins, one of them, as usual upon large plantations in the South, being a negro—a fellow of infinite excellence in drawing the bow. The other was an amiable young gentleman of the neighbourhood, whose good nature and real merits as a musician, led him frequently to perform at the friendly reunions in the Parish. Between the two we had really first rate fiddling; and the carpets soon disappeared from the hall and the opposite apartment to the parlour, affording ample room and verge enough for our purposes; and to it we went with a merry bound, and a perfect exhilaration of the soul, wheeling about in all the subdued graces of the quadrille, and forgetting phlegm and philosophy in a moment. The dancers were surrounded by the spectators, and, with Beatrice Mazyck as my partner, I confess to being as little disposed for grave thoughts and sober fancies, as any of my neighbours.

Your country ball is quite a different sort of thing from that of the fashionable city. It is more distinguished by *abandon*. There is a less feeling of restraint in the one situation than the other. Nobody is critical, there are few or no strangers, not sufficient to check mirth or irritate self-esteem, and the heels fairly take entire possession of the head. I had not been in such a glow for months. I had not conjectured the extent of my own agility, and Beatrice swam through the circle, proudly and gracefully, as the Queen of Sheba, over the mirrored avenues (according to the Rabbinical tradition) of Solomon.

"You are a lucky dog, Dick," whispered the Major in my ears. "Your partner is worthy to be an Empress. That scamp of a son of mine, he has possessed himself of that little French devil, in spite of all I could say. Just look at her, what a little, insignificant thing she is—yet she can dance—but that is French, of course. See how she whirls—egad! she *can* dance—she goes through the circle like a bird. But to dance well, Dick, don't make the fine woman! No! no! Deuce take the fellow that has no eyes for a proper object."

I was whirled away at this moment, but when I got back to my place, he was there still, continuing his running commentary.

"Look at Mrs. Methuselah, there—the stiff embodiment of Gallic dignity in the days of Louis le Grand—I mean, Madame Agnes-Theresa. Oh! she's a beauty. See how she smiles and simpers, as if she thought so herself. I suppose, however, it's only her pride that's delighted at the fine evolutions of her little French apology for a woman. And see, Ned, the rascal—he sees

7*

nobody but her. He does not dream that I am watching him all the while. I fancy, by the way, he does not greatly care! But I'll astonish him yet, Dick, you shall see! If he vexes me, I'll marry again, by all that's beautiful!"

Well might the soul of Ned Bulmer be ravished out of his eyes. Paula Bonneau is certainly the most exquisite little fairy on the wing in a ball-room, that ever eye-sight strove in vain to follow. Never sylph wandered or floated along the sands under the hallowing moon-light and the breathing spells of the sweet south, with a more witchlike or bewitching motion. She was the observed of all observers; and it was a perfect study itself, appealing to the gentle and amiable heart, to behold the rapt delight in her stiff old grand dame's eyes, as she followed her little figure everywhere through the mazes of the dance. At that moment, the old lady's heart was in good humour with all the world. She even smiled on Major Bulmer as he approached, though, the instant after, meeting with a profound and stately bow from him, she drew herself up to her full height, lifted her fan slowly, with measured evolutions before her face, and seemed to be counting the number of lustres in the chandelier.

"What a conceited, consequential old fool!" muttered the Major, as he passed onward. "Strange! that poor old French woman actually persuades herself that she is a human being, and of really the fairest sort of material."

Had he heard the unspoken comment of Madame Girardin at the same moment upon himself!

"It is certainly very singular that you can never make a gentleman of an Englishman. Physically, they are certainly well made people, next to the French. Mentally, they are capable in sundry departments. They are undoubtedly brave, and, if the French were extinct, might be accounted the bravest of living races. They have wealth and numerous old families, but all derived from the Norman French. Still, there is a something wanting, without which there can be no grace or refinement. They have the manners of oxen,—Bulls,—hence the name of John Bull, the propriety of which they themselves acknowledge. You cannot make them gentlemen by any process."

But these mutual snarlers and satirists did not disturb the progress of the ball. My next partner was Paula Bonneau. I looked to see with whom Ned Bulmer had united his dancing destinies, curious to ascertain how far he was disposed to comply with the wishes of his father; but he was no where that I could see, while Beatrice might be beheld floating away like a swan with my friend, Gourdin. The Major came up to me in one of the pauses of the drama.

"That cub of mine," says he, "has let the game escape him again. I could wring his neck for him. He is now hopping it with Monimia Porcher,—dancing with every body but the person with whom I wish him to dance. What does he not deserve !"

And so the time passed till the short hours wore towards ; and then between 12 and 1, the supper signal was given, when we all marched into the basement. I had secured the arm of Beatrice Mazyck in the procession ; and when I entered the supper saloon, conspicuous near the head of the table was Ned Bulmer, supplying the plate of Paula Bonneau. The Major saw him at the same moment, and was evidently no longer able to control his chagrin. He looked all sorts of terrors. Mars never wore fiercer visage on a frosty night. His fury lost him his supper, but he drank like a Turk in secret. Beaker after beaker of rosy champagne was filled and emptied, and when I returned up stairs with my fair companion, I left him with the young men still busy below at the bottle. When he came above, which was some half an hour after, he abruptly strode across the parlour to the spot where Ned was still in attendance upon Paula.

"Come, sir," said he, "if you mean to drive me home to-night.

I am ready—and your buggy is ready, sir,—I have already ordered it."

Ned was disquieted at the summons, but he quickly saw that the old man's nerves were disordered by the wine, and the filial duty of the son became instantly active, prompting him to take him off, lest other eyes should see his condition as clearly as his own. He said cheerfully—

"I am also ready, sir, and will only make my bow to Mrs. Mazyck."

"Bow be ——!" muttered the Major. "You've been bowing it all night with a vengeance."

This was scarcely heard by more than the son and myself. His sister, Miss Bulmer, upon whom I was in attendance, now came up.

"Brother," said she, "hadn't you better take a seat with us in the carriage, and let Ned drive home with Tony only."

"And why, pray," he responded sharply, "should I change any of my plans? Am I so old as to need back supporters and cushions? or do you fear that I shall catch rheumatism? Rheumatism never ran in my family. No! no! I drive home as I came—in the buggy."

There was no more to be said. The Major, giving himself a fair start, crossed the room to Mrs. Mazyck and Beatrice, and to each severally, in the deliberate style of King Charles's courtiers, made his elaborate bow, the right foot thrown back and toe turned out, as the base of the operation, and the left foot drawn with a sweep, so as to lodge its heel almost within the inner curve of the right: arms describing the well known half circle, and body bent forward, so as to enable the hands, if they so wished it, to rest upon the knees. And the operation was over, and Ned and sire passed out of sight, leaving Miss Bulmer in my charge. We did not linger long after. I had a few more sweet words to exchange with Beatrice—who treated me, evidently, with a greater degree of kindness than her good mother was prepared to smile upon—and to roll forth sundry sentences of rotund compliment to Madame Agnes-Theresa, upon the performances of Paula, whose bright eyes returned their acknowledgments for a very different sort of service. They took their departure before us, and I saw them to the carriage. It appears that Mrs. Mazyck had some private words with Miss Bulmer, and detained her after the departure of most of the guests. Of course, I did not scruple to enjoy a corresponding *tête-a-tête* with Beatrice, and had no complaints to make of the delay. This was much shorter than I could have wished, and, all too soon, I found myself in the carriage with Miss Bulmer, and hurrying off for "The Barony." Before we reached that place, however, other adventures were destined to occur, and those of a sort to require a chapter to themselves.

CHAPTER XI.

WHAT TURNS UP ON A DRIVE, AND WHO TURNS OVER.

To drive by night, two or four in hand, through our dim but picturesque avenues of pine, faintly lighted only by moon or stars, is an operation that is apt to try the nerves and skill of the city bred Jehu, accustomed only to broad streets, under the full blaze of gas lamps every fifty yards. But to the country gentleman, the thing is as familiar as one's garter, and without a thought of accidents, he will start for home at midnight, the darkest night, or drive to a frolic five or ten miles off, and never give the mere compassing of that distance a moment's consideration. Persons bred in the country see farther and better than citizens. So do sailors. Neither of these classes, accustomed to broad and spacious land and water scopes, is ever troubled with the infirmity of nearsightedness. This belongs wholly to city life, where the eye, from the earliest period, is made familiar to certain bounds, high-walled streets and contracted chambers. A faculty grows from its use and exercise, and is more or less enfeebled by *non-user*. The eye, tasked only within certain limits, loses the capacity to extend its range of vision when the occasion requires it. The muscles contract, and the shape of the eye itself undergoes a change corresponding immediately with the sort of use which is given it. But, I digress.

Exercised in the woods, night and day, the country gentleman never hesitates about the darkness, and starts for home, at all hours. Nobody, therefore, leaving the party at Mrs. Mazyck's, between one and two in the morning, ever regarded the lateness of the hour as a reason for not departing. Some few old ladies remained at Mazyck Place all night. The rest, in backwoods parlance, '*put out*,' as soon as supper was fairly over. Some had a mile or two only to go, and others found quarters among the neighbours, as is the custom of the country everywhere in the South. Others pushed on for home, and some few went probably eight or ten miles. We had barely five to go, and counted it as nothing. The night was clear but dark. The stars gave but a faint light, sprinkling their pale beams upon us through crowding tree tops. The young moon had gone down early; but the horses knew the way as well as the driver, or better, and were bound homewards. Ours was a negro driver, and one of that class, with owl faculty and visage, which sees rather better in the night than the day. It was this faculty, rather than his personal beauty, which secured for Jehu—that was really his name—the honourable place of coachman to Miss Bulmer. Off we went spinningly, whirling out of the court and into the open road at a keen pace, which promised to bear us home in short order. Miss B., well wrapped up, occupied the back seat of the carriage. I took my place with Jehu, preferring a mouthful of the cool, bracing air of morning. Merrily danced the pines beside us,—oaks nodded to us, doffing their green turbans as we sped; now we rolled through a little sand hill, now we dashed the waters up from the bottom of a sandy brooklet. The faint light of the stars gives a strange, wild beauty to such a scene and drive, and I was lost in mixed meditations, in which groves were found pleasantly convenient, and through which I caught glimpses of a damsel, well veiled, coming to meet me, when I was disturbed in my reveries by Jehu suddenly pulling up the horses, and coming to a dead halt.

"What's the matter, Jehu?"

"There's a break down here, sir," quoth he, calling to the boy to descend, who rode behind the carriage,—"Go look, boy, see what's happen."

I could now distinguish a carriage ahead, and a confused group beyond it. A lantern was borne in the hands of some person who seemed moving with it across the road. Of course, I leapt down in a moment, and, begging Miss Bulmer to keep quiet, and bidding Jehu keep back, I went forward to see into the extent of the misfortune, and ascertain who were the sufferers by it. This was quickly known;—but, perhaps, I had better go back in my history, and report the progress of those whom the matter most concerned. I give particulars, now, which I gathered subsequently from certain of the parties.

It appears that, from the moment of starting with his son, Major Bulmer began reproaching him with his conduct during the evening, and his neglect of Miss Mazyck. He barely suffered the buggy to get out of the court yard and into the main road, when his indignation broke forth into angry words.

"Well, sir; and how do you propose to excuse your conduct this evening."

"My conduct, sir? I don't understand you. I really flattered myself that I had been doing the handsome thing all the evening, making myself very agreeable all round, and certainly finding a great deal that was greatly agreeable to myself."

"You are a puppy, sir, and a fool, with your self-complaisance. I can tell you that, sir."

"Choice epithets, certainly, and very complimentary."

"Well, sir, you deserve them. Why do you provoke me?"

"You provoke yourself, father. Speaking reasonably, sir, I see nothing of which you can properly complain in my conduct."

"Indeed, sir; and who, pray, taught you to speak reasonably. No man, sir, speaks reasonably, unless he thinks rationally."

"A logical conclusion, truly."

"So it is,—and no man who acts like a fool, can be held a reasoning animal."

"True, again, logically."

"I say, sir, you are a dolt, a mere driveller, committing suicide morally, and striving against those who would help you out of deep water."

"Who would drown me rather—deny me the privilege to swim in the places which I most prefer."

"Hear me, Ned Bulmer,—why do you not listen to what I'm saying?"

"I have been listening, sir, very patiently. Go ahead!"

"Go ahead! Why will you, sir, knowing your family and breeding, indulge in those vile samples of Western slang? Speak like a gentleman, sir, even if you do not understand how to behave like one!',

Ned said nothing, gave the horse the goad, and waited for the next volley.

"Well, sir; after what I said to you on our way to Mrs. Mazyck's,—after a full showing to you of what I desired—what did you mean, sir, by so entirely slighting my wishes?"

"Your wishes were not mine, sir," answered Ned very coolly, "and even if they were, sir, a ball room, though a very good place for a flirtation, is not exactly the scene for a *bona fide* courtship."

"I may grant you that, sir, but I did not ask that you would

would make it the scene of a courtship. I only asked that you would offer such civilities and attentions to Miss Mazyck,—"

" As she, her mother, and everybody else might construe to mean courtship."

" You will oblige me not to finish my sentences for me, sir. I say, Edward Bulmer, that you were not even decently civil to Mrs. Mazyck and daughter."

" There I must deny you, sir. The matter is one of opinion. I contend that I was as civil, considerate and respectful in my attentions to both the ladies, as the elder had a right to require, and the younger desired to receive."

" And how know you, sir, what the younger desired to receive ?"

" By infallible instincts. The fact is, father, it is of no use to trouble me or yourself in regard to Beatrice Mazyck. I assure you, sir, that every body sees, if you do not, that another man has won her heart."

" You mean Dick Cooper."

" I do."

" Well, sir, I have Dick's assurance, from his own lips, that there have been no love passages between them ; that they are entirely uncommitted to each other."

" And no doubt what Dick told you, sir, is perfectly true ; but things have changed since your day, sir. People have become more refined and less formal. It don't need, now-a-days, to make a declaration in words in order to be understood. In your day, when all gentlemen were moulded upon one model, and all affections spoke through one medium, and after a particular form— when, in fact, the affections were not recognized at all—and when father or mother could swap off their children as the condition by which alone they could unite certain acres of swamp and uplands,— such an intercourse as that of Beatrice Mazzyck and Dick Cooper would pass for nothing. *Mais, nous avons changé tout cela !*"

" Ah ! d—n that gibberish. Speak in English if you will speak.

8

Though, by the way, speaking such consummate nonsense and stuff as you do, perhaps French is the proper dialect. Well, sir, what more ;—use what lingo you please."

"Oh! sir, any thing to please *you*. I have few more words to say; and I do say, that, though no words may have been exchanged between Beatrice Mazyck and Dick Cooper on the subject, yet their hearts, sir, are as irrevocably engaged, as if the Reverend Mr. Hymen, of the old Greek Church, had been called in to officiate. Hearts, sir, have a language in *our* day, which was denied them in yours. Perhaps this is one of the redeeming features of ultra democracy!"

"You have talked a long farrago of nonsense, Edward Bulmer, in which, as far as I can perceive, you have aimed at nothing more than to accumulate together all those topics which, in their nature, might offend me. I will meditate this hereafter. To make my complaints of your conduct more specific, why, sir, did you attach yourself the whole evening to the Bonneau faction, neglecting wholly Mrs. Mazyck and her daughter."

"Your charge is not more specific now than before. It is quite as easily answered. I join issue with you on the fact, sir."

"What, do you question my word?"

"No, sir, by no means,—only the correctness of your opinion."

"Sir, it is a matter of mere testimony. I beheld it with my own eyes."

"Your eyes deceived you, father."

"How, sir? Did you not dance repeatedly with Miss Bonneau?"

"I did, sir."

"Did you ever dance *once* with Miss Mazyck?"

"I did *not*, sir."

"Well, sir;—yet you persist that you were attentive to the latter lady."

"I do, sir, as far as it was possible. I proposed to dance with her, and she was engaged. This sir, on two occasions—quite often enough, I think, to try a lady's mood towards you."

"Edward Bulmer, is it possible that you resort to evasion! Sir, I know too well what is the practice with young men, where they wish to escape a duty. In my day, sir, and I confess I was guilty of this conduct myself, it was not unfrequently the trick—*trick*, I I say, sir, *trick!*—to ask a lady *after* she was *known* to be engaged for the coming set. Now, sir, answer me honestly, was not this *your* trick, sir, on this occasion."

"A practice deemed honourable in your day, cannot surely be regarded as discreditable; and I have now only to plead your own example, sir, if I desired to escape your anger. But, in truth, sir, I did not, on any occasion, *know* that Miss Mazyck was engaged to another partner when I asked."

"But you conjectured it, sir,—you kept off untill the last moment, sir. You well know that Beatrice Mazyck is not likely to hang as a wall-flower, and you gave everybody the desired opportunity, sir. Edward Bulmer, it was a mere mockery of Miss Mazyck, to solicit her hand when you did."

"She, I fancy, was very well pleased with that sort of mockery."

"Sir, did you *ever*, *on any one occasion*, offer yourself to her for the second or third dance, when she pleaded previous engagement. That, sir, is a common custom with young gentlemen—is it not."

"Yes, sir,—and one more honoured in the breach than the observance. I don't approve of it myself, and don't encourage it in others."

"You don't, eh! Well, sir, I made you a special request that you would see Miss Mazyck to the supper-table. Why did you not?"

"Dick Cooper was before me, sir."

"Dick Cooper before you! Yes, indeed, he will go before you all your life; That man will be somebody yet. Not a mere Jehu or Jockey, sir.   He will not waste his life among the pumpkins.   I would to God he could drive into your empty noddle some of that good sense and proper veneration which distinguish himself."

" Well, sir, you will admit that if I'm unworthy of Miss Mazyck, he is not."

" Who says you are unworthy, sir ?"

" My humility, sir."

" D——n your humility.   I wish you knew how to exercise it in the right place.   You are a puppy and a scrub, and fit only for such a petty little French popinjay as that—"

" Stop now, father, or I'll be sure to upset you!   If you speak disrespectfully of Paula Bonneau, you will certainly so outrage my nervous sensibility, that I shall turn the buggy over into the first bramble bush that I see; and then, sir, you'll be in the condition of the man who lost both his eyes in a similar situation.   You remember the pathetic ditty—

> " And when he saw his eyes were out,
>   With all his might and main,
>   He jump'd into another bush,
>   And scratch'd 'em in again."

But that feat's not to be performed every day.   You might try from bush to bush between here and home, and fail to scratch back your pupils."

" Pshaw—you blockhead!   But where the deuce are you driving, sir?   You are out of the road."

" No, sir,—I am in the road far enough.   I confess I'm on the look-out for the briar patch; and should I see one,———"

" Zounds, man, you are out of the road.   I see the track to the left."

" No, sir, it runs to the right.   I see it well enough.   Don't touch the reins, sir,—you'll do mischief."

" Do mischief!   You would teach your grandmother how to eat her eggs, would you?   Teach me to drive!   You would provoke a saint, Ned Bulmer! Give me the reins, or you will have us in the woods."

"Fear nothing, sir; I see exactly where I am going. I see the road perfectly, every step of it!"

"You see nothing, sir, I tell you, but your own perverse disposition to foil me in every thing. If I did not know, sir, that you are a temperate man, I should suspect you of taking quite too much champagne to-night"

Ned Bulmer could not resist the disposition to chuckle.

"What do you mean by that laugh, sir? There, again,—you will have us in the woods. It is either your hands that are unsteady, or it is your horse that shies?"

"Isn't it barely possible, sir, that it is the stars that shy?" was the response of Ned, conveying thus what was designed to be a very sly insinuation. But the Major's faculties had not been so much bedevilled as his eye sight. He caught the equivocal import of the suggestion in a moment.

"Really, sir, this is most insolent. You are drunk, sir, positively drunk, and will break both our necks, in this atrocious buggy. Give me the reins, I tell you."

"Hold off, father," cried the son earnestly; "we are going right. There is no danger, but the road here is narrow and the fence on the left is pretty close."

"Fence on the left! Where the d—l do you see any fence on the left? Where do you think we are, sir?"

This was the first time that Ned suspected that his father's sight was becoming bad. He knew not whether to ascribe it to his own age, or that of the wine.

"At Gervais's corner."

"Pshaw! we have passed it long ago. You are in no condition to drive. That's plain enough."

With the words he grasped one of the reins furiously, whirled the tender-mouthed grey round before Ned could guard against the

8*

proceeding, and in a moment, striking the corner of the rail fence, the buggy was turned over, and the horse off with it. The Major made a sudden evolution in the air and came down heavily against the fence. Ned was pitched in among the pines, on the opposite side of the road, and both lay for a time insensible.

CHAPTER XII.

A GROUP ON THE HIGHWAY.   A NEW STUDY FOR THE PAINTER.

It is not yet known how long the father and son lay in this condition before they received assistance. They were first discovered by the coachman of Madame Agnes-Therese Girardin, as he drove that lady and her grand-daughter slowly home from the ball.

" Wha' dis yer ?" quoth Antony, the coachman. " I see some-t'ing in de road."

" What do you see, Antony ?" demanded the lady.

" I yer somebody da grunt," quoth Tony. " He's a pusson— (person)—he's a man for certain."

" A man in the road, groaning !" said the old lady. " Peter ! Peter !"—to the boy riding behind. Antony drew up his horses at a full stop. Peter jumped down and came forward.

" Take one of the lamps, Peter, and see who is lying in the road."

The urchin moved promptly, and, hurrying forward, stooped over one of the victims, holding the light close to his face. He came back instantly.

" Its Mass Ned Bullimer, missis."

" Mr. Edward Bulmer !" said the ancient lady, and she hemmed thrice and began violently to agitate—her fan.

" Edward !—Edward Bulmer !" cried the young lady, almost

with a scream, beginning violently to agitate—herself. "Oh! *mamma*, let us get out and see. He is hurt. He is killed."

"No, Miss Paula, he aint dead yet,—he da grunt." This was meant to be consolatory.

"Be quiet, Paula, my child; do not excite yourself—we will see—we will inquire. But—"

"Open the door, Peter!" cried Paula, with an energy and resolution which she did not ordinarily exhibit, and of which the old lady did not altogether approve, though the occasion was one which did not allow of any deliberation. Peter, meanwhile, opened the door of the carriage, and the young lady darted out.

"Stay, Paula, stay, till I get my cologne, and—"

But the damsel was off, and a bound brought her to the side of her lover, stretched out partly upon the road, his shoulder resting against a pine sapling. She knelt beside him, called to him with the tenderest accents, and was answered by a groan. These groans were signs of returning consciousness, at once to suffering and life. Meanwhile, the good grandmother had hobbled out, and approached the scene of action; a bottle of cologne water in one hand and her vinaigrette in the other.

"Rub his head, my daughter, and sprinkle him with cologne; hold this vinaigrette to his nostrils, and tell him to snuff."

Another groan, and then the maiden heard him in faint accents say—"My father—see—my father."

"His father! Oh! Major Bulmer," quoth the old lady. "Yes, they went away together."

"In de buggy, missis," interposed the knowing Peter. He himself had opened the gate for the buggy, and had received a shilling for his attentions.

"Look for him, Peter," said the old lady—and she muttered to herself, as if to justify her humanity, "He is one of God's creatures, at least; it is our Christian duty only." And with these words she followed Peter in his search.

The Major was found in the fence corner, lying partly across one of the *stakes,* which his weight had broken, his head striking against a rail. The old lady was quite terrified when she beheld him. His head had been cut, an ugly gash, ranging from the upper part of one ear to the temples. He was still bleeding freely. Antony was immediately summoned to bring the other lamp of the carriage, while Peter was made to mount one of the horses, in order to ride back for Dr. Porcher, who was at the party, and who, it was hoped, might be still found there. Madame Agnes-Therese, in the meanwhile, to her credit be it said, forgetting old prejudices and antipathies, forgetting all forms and restraints, and stiffnesses and formalities, kneeling beside the insensible Major, proceeded to staunch the blood and close the wound. She had lived a long time in the world, and had acquired much of that household practical knowledge and dexterity which enables one to be useful in almost any emergency. And she pursued her present labour with a good deal of skill and success. The vinaigrette and the cologne were passed from patient to patient, as they severally seemed most to need it. Antony was despatched to the *branch,* or brooklet, which they had passed only a few moments before, to bring his carriage bucket full of water. The faces of the two were sprinkled with water, cologne poured into their mouths, and both seemed to revive about the same time. The first words of the father were significant of quite a different feeling from that which he exhibited during the unlucky drive.

"Ned, my dear boy; Ned, are you hurt?"

The old lady, holding the lamp up to his face, endeavoured to press him down, in order to keep him quiet.

"Do not speak; do not agitate yourself, Major Bulmer; your son is doing well. He is not much hurt—not much, I assure you—I, Mrs. Girardin."

"Heh!—you—Mrs. Gi——."

He resolutely sate up, in spite of all her efforts, and stared her in the face with a countenance in which surprise was so extreme as almost to seem horror. Fancy the spectacle. Madame Girardin holding the carriage lamp with one hand, kneeling on one knee, and with the other hand striving to press the old gentleman backwards. He, now sitting, his arms supporting him in the position, with his hands resting on the ground; and staring with such a face into her own. He had almost recovered his senses quite, and astonishment had partly overcome his pain. It was at this moment, and while the expression was still upon his visage, that our carriage drew up to the scene of the accident. We necessarily halted also, soon got out, and almost as soon learned all the particulars. In a moment after, Dr. Porcher arrived, fortunately having met Peter on the route, and proceeded to examine into the condition of the sufferers.

The evil was not so serious as we had at first reason to apprehend. The real sufferer was Ned Bulmer, whose left arm was broken, and who was otherwise considerably bruized about the body. The Major had an acre of bruizes, according to his own phrase, over back and shoulders and sides. But, excepting the ugly gash over his temple, there was nothing to disquiet him for more than a week. But he had a narrow escape. The skull was uninjured, but a little more obliquity in his fall would have crushed it. As it was, the wound was really only skin deep; but it left an ugly scar forever after, which, as a fine-looking man, who had always been particularly well satisfied with his visage, occasioned the proprietor many and frequent regrets.

But we must take our groups out of the highway. The arm of Ned Bulmer was temporarily bandaged, and we lifted him into the carriage with as much tenderness as possible. This carriage was Madame Girardin's. The moment she discovered that each of the wounded men would require two seats, she graciously accorded the use of her vehicle. Of the two, she perhaps preferred the son to the father as an inmate; but dear little Paula, clinging to her lover tenaciously, disposed of the matter without leaving any thing to the option of the grandmother; and, at her requisition, as soon as Ned was fully restored to consciousness, the Doctor, myself and Antony, lifted him in, not a little helped by Paula. The same service rendered to the Major, and the Doctor led the way in his own vehicle. We drove slowly, and day was dawning as we entered the court. The patients were carefully taken out, put to bed, and more methodically and scientifically attended to. But before Madame Girardin departed, and as she was preparing to do so, the Major begged to see her in his chamber.

"Mrs. Girardin, I am too feeble and sore to rise, but you will believe me, as feeling very deeply and warmly your kindness and the succour which you rendered to my son and myself."

To which the old lady replied :—

"Major Bulmer, you will please believe that I am grateful to God in permitting me to be of any help to any of his creatures."

When she had departed, the Major said :—

"Well, I owe the old lady my gratitude. She has good stuff in her, though she is of French stock."

The old lady had her comment also, muttered to Paula as she rode :—

"If Major Bulmer did not sometimes make himself so offensive by his pride,—his Bull family pride,—he might yet be made a gentleman."

I must not omit to mention that, while the grandmother visited the father, the grand-daughter visited the son; but what was said between the two latter, has never, that I know of, been reported to any third person.

CHAPTER XIII.

THE PROGRESS OF DOMESTIC REVOLUTION.

The misadventure, happening so near to Christmas—that sea son when we require to have all our limbs in perfection, our bodies free from bruises, and our spirits buoyant over all restraints,—was the great subject of annoyance with the Major. Christmas was assigned by him for a great festival—a something more than was customary in the country, in which every body that was any body, was to be at the Barony. The accident happened on the 13th of December. But twelve days, accordingly, were allowed to the sufferers to get well. With respect to the Major himself, this, perhaps, bating the scar upon the forehead, was not a matter of much doubt or difficulty. But the case was otherwise with poor Ned, whose arm, the Doctor affirmed, could not be suffered to go free of splint and sling under a goodly month. What a month of vexation. So, at least, it seemed. But the good grows out of the evil, even as the cauliflower out of the dunghill. Evil, according to the ordinance, is the moral manure for good. The Major lost something of his imperious will in the feelings of self-reproach which seized upon him. He now beheld, what he did not then, that it was the champagne which he had imbibed, and not that which he had imputed to his son, that had tumbled the pair into the pathway. He also began to suspect, what Ned would never have hinted to him, that age was giving certain premonitions in the shape of a failing eye-sight. Strange that he had never seen that fence. Was it the wine or the years? Both, perhaps. This conclusion humbled the old man. He sought the chamber of his son.

"My dear boy," he said, "I won't ask you to forgive me, for such a request will give you more pain, I know, than any thing besides; but I feel that it is not easy to forgive myself. I had drank

too much champagne, that is certain.   But I was angry with you,
Ned,—and you know what one of our modern poets says :—

> " And to be wroth with those we love,
>   Doth work like madness in the brain."

I am not sure that I quote literally, but I am pretty near it.   I
could not eat, and drank freely on an empty stomach.   This made
me wilful; and Ned, my boy, you provoked me.   You were a little too cool,—too cavalier.   Had you drank freely too—had you
been angry or quarrelsome—all would have gone right.   But, no
matter now.   It does not help to go over the same ground again."

   " No," quoth Ned, between a writhe and a smile, a grin and a
contortion, not able to resist the temptation—" More likely to
hurt—perhaps the other *eye*, the other *arm*."

   " Well," good humoredly responded the Major, "you are doing
well, so long as you can perpetrate a pun."

   " Of old, you held that to be doing *ill*."

   " What! another! Dick,"—to me—" is he not incorrigible!
But, Ned, my boy, you must hurry your proceedings.   It won't
do to have you laid up at Christmas.   Get well as fast as you can,
and, as an inducement, I have sent to town already, to Reynolds,
ordering a new buggy.   Your horse is badly hurt in the flanks.   I
must take him off your hands.   You shall have two hundred dollars for him, or the pick of any draught horse in my stable—they
are all *free*."

   " I'll take the money, papa.   I have suffered too much from
your *free draughts*."

   " What a propensity. But I forgive you, considering your arm."

   " Strange, too, that I should owe my safety to that which I can
no longer count *upon*."

   " A *pun* again! I give you up.   But look at my phiz.   Am I
in a condition to call upon Madame Agnes-Theresa this morning?"

   Ned looked up with some curiosity—anxiety perhaps—in his

glance. We both agreed that the scar had an honourable appearance.

"Ah!" quoth the Major, I should not have been ashamed of it had it been won in battle—driving an enemy instead of driving a horse."

"At the head of the *Fencibles,* instead of the foot of the *fence,*" murmured Ned languidly.

"You did serve in the war of 1815, Major," was my remark.

"Yes, after a fashion, along the sea coast; but we never had any encounter with the enemy. Their shipping lay in sight of the coast, and their boats sometimes put into the creeks and rivers, but they fought shy of us."

"Knowing, perhaps, that they would have to deal with *shy* fighters," quoth Ned.

"No, indeed. We were brave enough, under the circumstances. Once we thought we had a chance. It was after night, but starlight; the tide was coming in, and one of our sentinels discovered a boat making straight for shore. We crouched among the sands, flat on our faces, making ready. When within gun shot, we poured in a terrific fire and rushed up to finish the work with the bayonets. We found the boat riddled admirably with our balls, but nothing in her but a junk bottle and a jacket, and both empty. She had drifted from the Lacedemonian man-of-war. Her capture was thought no small evidence of our prowess, showing how we could have fought. The Charleston papers were particularly eloquent in our praise, and I'm not sure but salutes were fired from Castle Pinckney in our honour. It was no fault of ours that the British feared us too greatly to venture any soldiers in the skiff. That was our only achievement, unless I mention a somewhat ineffectual fire at a barge, about seven miles off. It is barely possible that the enemy saw the smoke of our muskets. They could not have heard the report. But, you think I will do to see Madame Girardin?"

" As well as any gallant of us all," was my reply.

" Very good. I'll ride over this morning."

" Eyes right, father, and look out for fences on the left."

" Get out, you dog. Trust me, never again to take champagne or any other liquor on an empty stomach."

" And, beware of the black dog, father."

" The tiger is becoming pacified, Ned," was my remark after the departure of the Major. " He has had a bad scare. He will come round by degrees. All the symptoms are favourable."

" He will give up some favourite projects then. His heart has been more earnestly set on this marriage than I had suspected. I am now convinced he has been planning it for months, and I have reason to believe that he opened the subject to Mrs. Mazyck before she went to travel last summer. He is tenacious of such matters."

" No doubt ; and without some extraordinary event he would have continued so. This accident has been a great good fortune. The Major has too uniformly escaped successfully from those evils to which flesh is heir. Uninterrupted good fortune is quite too apt to harden the hearts of the very best men. They finally believe themselves to be entitled to impunity. It requires a disaster to rebuke arrogance ; and one should pray for an occasional mischance, knowing our tendency to self-reliance. We must every now and then receive a lesson which teaches us that God is still the Ruler of the Universe, and that the richest, the strongest, the bravest, the wisest, are but feathers and straw before his breath. Your father has just had one of these excellent lessons. He has been taught the exceeding shortness of the step between an imperial will, a haughty temper, a glorious future, and suffering, agony, the grave, the loss of the thing most precious, the overthrow of the most cherished pride and vanity. You are the only son, and the very will which threatened to wreck your hopes, was based upon the desire to subserve your success and prosperity.

Strange as it may seem, parents are thus constantly employed, at once for the good and the mortification of their children. Keep up your spirits. Do not vex him. Say nothing of your hurts. He will see them, and suppose them, fast enough; and your very forbearance to complain will, in his mind, exaggerate the amount of your suffering. There will be a degree of remorse at work within his bosom, which shall impel his moods hereafter in an entirely opposite direction."

" But, you do not augur any thing from this visit to Madame Girardin ?"

" By no means. As a gentleman, he could do no less. He had to go. There is no merit in the act. He owes the old lady and the young one the visit, and something more. But, there is something favourable in the fact that he does it willingly, cheerfully, and with a grace, showing that the duty is now by no means an irksome one. A week ago, and to be required to visit the Bonneau plantation would have been like taking a pill of myrrh and aloes."

Let us follow the Baron, and see the issue of his visit.

When it was announced to Madame Girardin that Major Bulmer was in the parlour, she was quite in a fidget. " Bonita," her own maid, a mulatto of Cuban origin, and " Marie," the waiting maid of Paula, were both summoned.

"Bonita, what has become of my mantua cap ? Marie, I told you to put away my Valenciennes. Dear me, Paula, I can find nothing, and these servants are positively in the way of each other. They are certainly the most awkward and useless creatures in the world. Paula, child, do look into your drawers for the Valenciennes tippet. Ah! there it is. Paula, child, do fix me,—pin the cap for me, and put on that bunch of crimson ribbons. Crimson always suited my hair best, and complexion. Do get away, Bonita—you only disorder me. You are getting quite too fat and clumsy for any useful purpose about house. I'll have to send you into the field. Heavens, what will Major Bulmer say to being kept so long? Why, Paula, where are you, child?"

Paula was already down stairs. Madame Agnes-Theresa was still a long time fixing. For years she had never taken such pains to caparison herself for any encounter with the other gender. Strange! that she should be so solicitous about her personal appearance, when she was to meet with one whom she had always regarded with prejudice and the bitterest hostility. Yet, not strange! Oh! woman, after all, claim what you please for yourself; assert what rights you please; estimate your charms at the highest; pride yourself as you may upon your intrinsic worth; suppose yourself, if you please, of the purest and most precious porcelain clay that ever afforded materials for celestial manufacture;— then, put what rough estimate you may on man—suppose him all that is rude, and wild, and rough, and tough,—all dough and mortality if you think proper,—a mere savage in beaver and breeches,—a mere beast of burden, with only half the usual allowance of legs and ears—still, my dear creature, all your painstaking are for him, even when he is of the rudest, and you the softest—all these careful caparisonings before the mirror,—all this assiduous training of the tresses—all this nice adjustment of the features,—the very disposition of that scarf and tippet, the careful twofold concealment and display of that white neck and bosom, that adroit placing of the jewel just where it is best calculated to inform him how much more precious is the jewel that hides beneath,—that confining zone,—that flowing drapery,—that bracelet spanning the snowy arm,—all, all,—the grace, the taste, the toil, the care, the smile, the motion,—all, all are designed to win his smile, to charm his fancy, provoke his admiration, compel his love. Talk of your rights! Confess the truth, for once, now, at this holiday season, and admit that the most precious of your rights, even in your own estimation, is that of winning his affection, wild colt, fierce tiger, beast of prey and burden as he is!

Dear, good, antique, frigid, stately, stiff, and bigoted Madame Girardin, was not superior to her sex; and this, by the way, my dear, is the one most precious jewel of her humanity. She was a good half hour in fixing, even after Paula Bonneau had descended to the parlour. The latter has gone down to meet the Major after the fashion of Nora Creina:

> " Oh! my Nora's gown for me,
>   That floats as wild as mountain breezes,
>   Leaving every beauty free,
>   To sink or swell as Heaven pleases.
>   Yes, my Nora Creina, dear,
>   My simple, graceful Nora Creina;
>   Nature's dress,
>   Is loveliness,
>   The dress you wear, my Nora Creina."

Never sticking a pin in her dress, never adjusting tippet or ribbon, the artless child bounded down to the meeting with Ned's father with a joyous, cheerful sentiment of delight and expectation. She knew that he would come,—that he was bound to come to make his acknowledgments,—but, somehow, there was a vague, undefinable feeling in her little heart, that his coming augured something more grateful,—something more positive than a mere formality. She fancied that the snows of winter were about to thaw, and, like a glad bird, she bounded forth with song to welcome in the first sunshine and the infant promise of the spring. And the old Major, bigoted and prejudiced, and feeling, as he did, that she stood in the way of one of his most cherished schemes in behalf of his son, he could not resist the child-like confidence, the unaffected and pure innocence of soul and spirit which displayed itself to his eye on her approach—so frank, so free, so joyous, the union of child and angel, so sweetly mingled in look and manner! She came towards him with extended hands, but he caught her in his arms, and kissed her, I fancy quite as affectionately as he would

9*

have done Beatrice Mazyck; then he put her from him at arm's length, and looked kindly into her large, bright, dewy eyes.

"Oh! I'm so glad to see you, and to see you well again, Major."

"My dear child, I owe it, perhaps, to you and to your good grandmother, that I am well again—or nearly so."

Paula did not disclaim the service, as many foolish people would do. She acted more wisely—said not a word about it; but looking at the scar, cried out, with child-like freedom :—

"But you have got a mark for life, Major. That was a terrible cut."

"Ah! my dear, but not half so severe as that which you would have made upon my heart, were I thirty years younger. As it is, I don't know how much love I do not owe you, old as I am."

And he took her again into his arms, and seated her upon his knees, and began to think that, after all, it was really not so strange that Ned Bulmer should take a fancy to the little damsel, though she was of that pernicious French stock. And the old man and the young girl prattled together like two children that have chased butterflies together, until the moment when that gem from the antique, Madame Girardin, strode into the apartment, looking very much like a crane on a visit of special ceremonial feeding, at the Court of the Frogs.

"Mrs. Girardin," quoth the Major, rising and making his famous bow, though at the cost of a few severe twitches of the back and arms,—"I come, my dear Madam, to return you my best thanks for your kindness and singular attention to myself and son, at a moment of very great pain and imminent danger to both. You acted the part, my dear Madam, of the good Samaritan, and when I think of the coldness of the night, your exposure on the damp earth, your fatigue, at an hour when repose was absolutely necessary,—the judicious efforts you employed, and the prompt intelligence which made you provide for immediate help,—I feel utterly at a loss for words to say how deeply I am penetrated by your kindness and benevolent consideration. I trust, my dear Mrs. Girardin, that you will receive my assurances in the spirit in which they are tendered, and that, hereafter, we shall become more to each other than mere passing acquaintances of the same parish."

The Major had evidently meditated this speech with a great deal of care. It betrayed cogitation, and this was its fault. His object was to express his feelings distinctly, and to declare his conviction of the friendly and useful assistance of the lady; yet without falling into formality. But, that he meditated at all, what he had to say, necessarily led him into formality. This is always the error with impulsive men, who forget that when impulse has become habitual, it has also become equally polished, proper and expressive. I am speaking now of educated people, of course. A man so impulsive as Major Bulmer, it is to be expected, must occasionally err in speech; but a man who is so free and frequent a speaker, is never apt to err very greatly, if he will leave himself alone, and wait for the promptings of the occasion. Had he, by accident, encountered Mrs. Girardin the morning after the accident, he would have thanked her in a single sentence and a look; and his gratitude would have seemed more decidedly warm from the heart, than it now declared itself.

But I am not so sure, remembering the sort of frigid person with whom he had to deal, that his present mode of address was not the most appropriate. It sounded dignified,—it appealed to her dignity. He made it an affair of state, and her state was accordingly lifted by it. It showed him deliberate in his approaches, even when his object was to give thanks, and this displayed his high sense of the service, and of the importance of the person addressed. All of which was rather grateful than otherwise to a person who still longed for the return of hoops and high head dresses. She answered him in similar fashion,—'She had done her duty only. We must give help to one another in the hour of distress and affliction. Major Bulmer's rank in society justified her departure from some of its strictnesses, in the effort to assist him. She was conscious of the impropriety, ordinarily, of stooping beside a gentleman, particularly on the high road; but she begged him to believe that, before she did so, she ascertained that he was actually insensible. She herself saw the blood streaming from his brows. She heard his groans. Otherwise, he was quite speechless. Under the circumstances, she had a Christian charity to fulfil. She thanked God she *was* a Christian,—true, a most unworthy one,—but she prayed nightly for Heavenly Grace to make her better. She was happy to believe that her prayers had been somewhat heard; assuming the very casualty of which the Major had been so nearly the victim, to be designed as affording her a special opportunity of serving one whom she had not been taught to recognize as a friend."

"Cool indeed," thought the Major. "Certainly very cool. I am to be upset by Providence, my own and son's neck perilled, only to afford her an opportunity to play the good Samaritan. Very cool, indeed!" thought the Major, though he suppressed the very natural comment. The self-complacency of the old lady now began to please him as a sort of study of character. But he spoke again. She had referred to his bloody appearance, to his groans unconsciously uttered. It was in something of the spirit of a certain Frenchman, of famous memory, that he said,—

"Really, Mrs. Girardin, when I was in that condition, I must greatly have disquieted you by my groans and shocking appearance. I am afraid I made some horrible wry faces. Believe me, my dear Madame, it was purely unintentional. Had I been conscious of your presence, I certainly would have constrained myself. I trust you did not construe my wry faces into any feeling of disapprobation at your presence, or the kindly succour you were giving me."

"No, sir; I thank God, who kept me from putting any such uncharitable construction on your conduct. Suffering as you did, in such a situation,—or had it been any body else,—I should have begged you to pay no attention to my presence, but to be as much at ease as possible !"

"At ease !" thought the Major. "What an idea !—what a strange woman." His spoken words were of another sort.

"I thank you, Mrs. Girardin,—from the bottom of my heart I thank you,—for myself and son. He, too, sends his thanks, though too great a sufferer to offer them in person. He will present himself as soon as he is able. To you, and this sweet angel of a daughter, we owe more than we can ever acknowledge."

To this, the good lady had a set speech, deprecating all acknowledgments. The delight of doing good was sufficient for her. To this the Major had his response ; to which the lady had hers ; the former replied again ; and Madam Agnes-Theresa answered him. By and by, the Major began to speak more at his ease, and, after a little while, making a prodigious leap from one point to another, he exclaimed abruptly :—

"The fact is, my dear Mrs. Girardin, we have been all our lives a couple of old fools—"

"Sir !"

"I beg pardon,—a thousand pardons. I meant to say that *I* have been a couple of old fools—not merely one fool—that would not answer to express my sense of my stupidity for so many years of my life. No, Madam, I have been a pair of fools; for living beside you in the parish so long, knowing your worth, and the honourable family to which you belong, yet never once seeking to show my estimation of it. It is thus, my dear Mrs. Girardin, that one will hunt for years after a treasure which is actually lying all the while in his path—that one will sigh and yearn after possessions for which he has only to open his eyes and stretch forth his hands,—and that we hourly lament the growing weakness, wickedness, and ignorance of the world around us, without being at the proper pains to welcome and value the good, the great, the wise and the virtuous, even when we find them. I have been a fool of this description of forty horse power. By God's blessing, my dear Mrs. Girardin, and, with your favour, I will show that I am recovering my senses. Permit me, then, to acknowledge my past stupidity in not knowing you better, and do not punish the offence, for which I feel a becoming remorse, by denying me permission to make proper amends in the future for the past."

Madame Agnes-Theresa was proud, and vain, and haughty, and clannish, and full of ridiculous notions of what was due especially to herself and family,—but she was not wilful or perverse. Properly appealed to, she was accessible, and, if she had no question of the sincerity of the offender, she was forgiving. Besides, as we have before hinted, her hostility to the Bulmer household arose from pique and a mortified spirit. She did not hold herself aloof from them, or toss her head haughtily when she heard them mentioned, because she felt her superiority over them, but simply because they seemed tacitly to assert theirs over her. Vain people are easily mollified. The very attempt to mollify them, soothes the self-esteem which you have outraged. Major Bulmer was a great beguiler of the sex. In his youth, a splendid figure, with a handsome face, he was irresistible. Even now, his figure was noble and erect, his eye open, manly, and of a glad, generous blue ; and his whole air was that of the born gentleman. Madame Girardin did not prove incorrigible. The signs of yielding were soon manifest, and when, pointing to an ancient portrait of a Knight in armour, hanging against the walls, the Major afforded her an opportunity of tracing the Girardin family to the fountain head which they were content to claim, he made a formidable advance into the champagne country of her affections. He put her on the right strain, and she told the story which he had heard from other sources a hundred times before, of that famous warrior, the Lord Paul St. Marc Girardin, who accompanied Saint Louis to the Holy

Land, and helped to bury him there. Then the old lady showed him the antique seal ring of the family, the crest being a cross-handled sword, the blade dividing a crescent at an awful swoop; then followed the narrative of the Lord Paul St. Marc's feats of arms, his prowess, the number of ladies he saved, hearts he won, Turks he slew. The Bonneaus, the old lady was pleased to admit, had never been quite so distinguished as the Girardins, but they, too, had done no small mischief upon Turks' heads and ladies' hearts. To slaughter foes, and jilt damsels, by the way, was, among the fine people fifty years ago, the two preferred processes for being honourably famous; and, with all her religion and bigotry, the good grandmother held rather tenaciously to the old faith in these performances.

And so the two talked away, and about the strangest things,— strangely communicative, for the first time in their lives, to one another, until, by the time the hour was ended,—you will scarce believe it, dutiful reader of mine, but it is a solemn and truthful chronicle which I indite,—but,—certainly I shall surprise you. Prepare yourself. What think you then? The old lady herself, Madame Agnes-Theresa, taking Major Bulmer by the arm, actu-ally conducted him out to look at a new smoke-house she had been building, and to show her new plans for curing hogs; then led him away, in the same style, to look at some new fowls of foreign va-rieties, roosters big as giraffes, and pullets that might have pacified Polyphemus, which her factor had bought for her at the great Fowl Fair in Charleston. "Fair is foul and foul is fair!" says Shakspeare, so that nobody need be offended at my present collo-cation of words. The Fowl Fair in Charleston had contributed largely to our grandmother's hen coop, and afforded material upon which the old lady and her guest could expatiate with equal elo-quence. Little Paula thought there would be no end of it; but the sly little puss, seeing that things were going rightly, never in-terposed an unnecessary word,—and her forbearance displayed eminent wisdom. Half the world are fools in this very particular. They put in an oar, just when the boat is making the best head-way, with tide, wind and current in favour, They stop the currents, they head the winds, and, in the effort to help progress, mar the enterprise forever. Keep your tongues, fools ; hold off your hands, donkies, and let " Go ahead " and " Do well," work their own passages, without clapping unnecessary steam to their tails.

" Well," quoth the old lady to Paula, after the Major had departed,—" well, my child, who would have thought it ! Who ever expected to see Major Bulmer in my house. Who ever listened to hear me welcome him ! There's some great change at hand, my child, when such things happen."

" The great change *has* happened, *mamma.*"

" Yes ; but it always betokens other changes yet. The Major has had a narrow escape. But he is old, and he may have suffered some secret injury, of which he never dreams. When people thus suddenly change in their dispositions, look for a singular change in their fortunes. Well, God be thanked for making him sensible, in his old age, and before it became too late, of what he owed to society and his neighbours. It is late, but not too late, and I pray that no evil consequences may follow the present change for the better in his disposition."

" How *can* it, *mamma ?*"

" Oh ! I don't know ; but change is an awful thing always, even when it happens for the better, and there is always some evil following in the footsteps of what is good. We must only hope and pray, and leave it all to heaven."

CHAPTER XIV.

WHICH AUGURS AN AFFAIR OF BOARS!

IT is the tendency of all revolutions, when they once fairly begin, to precipitate themselves with fearful rapidity. The impetus once given, and the car rolls onward, with a growing head of steam. The development is as eager as light in its progress, from the moment when the germinating principles begin to be active. It will be admitted that the transitive steps were soon overcome, in the overthrow of the ancient prejudices between the Bulmer and Bonneau families. Major Bulmer was a man of locomotive temperament, who could not well arrest himself in his own movement, having once begun it. Scarcely had he returned home, and reported what he had done, when he hurried to the library, in order to prepare billets of invitation for Madam Agnes-Theresa, and the fair Paula, to his proposed Golden Festival at Christmas. These performances were not so easy. Every precaution had to be taken by which to avoid offending the *amour propre* of the old lady and re-awakening her ancient prejudices. Twenty notes were begun, and were dismissed, because of some unlucky word or phrase. I was finally called in to the consultation, and required to prepare an epistle, possessing all the accuracy of a law paper, with all the blandness of a *billet doux*. Some hours were spent in devices, and doubts, and arguments, and objections, and quiddities, and quoddities, in order that we might not chafe rabidities and oddities. The work was done at length, but there was still a shaking of the head, on the part of the Major and Miss Bulmer, as to certain words, and dots, and consonants; and it was finally decreed that Ned should decide as to which, of half a dozen epistles, should be sent. The great, final consultation was held in his chamber,—and he decided,—and we may suppose with judgment,

10

concerning the result.   The billets were sent, for the old lady and her grand-daughter ; and before an answer could be received, Miss Bulmer,—a most benevolent and gentle soul as ever lived,—took the carriage and drove over to Madame Girardin, in order, if need be, to smooth over difficulties and overcome objections ; at all events, to add her eloquence to that of her brother, to persuade the parties to acceptance.   But, before her arrival, the discussion had taken place between the old lady and the grand-daughter.

"Well, Paula," quoth she, "wonders will never cease.   What do you think ?   Here is an invitation to me,—to me,—to spend Christmas day and night at Bulmer Barony.   And here is a note to yourself, I suppose, to the same effect."

And the old lady read her billet aloud, and then required the young one to re-read it, and to read her own.

"And now what do you say, my child.   Don't you think it very surprising ?"

"I don't see any thing to surprise us, mamma.   I confess it's only what I expected, after the Major's visit yesterday."

"Well! these sudden changes are very awful.   No one can tell what is to happen.   I declare they make me quite nervous.   Major Bulmer has never been on friendly terms with our family, but I think him a very worthy man, and I should be very sorry if any thing evil was to occur.   I knew once of a person who was a great sinner, a very wicked man, who swore like a trooper, and drank like a dragoon horse ; who was always quarrelling with somebody, and fighting and lawing with his neighbours ; who all at once became converted from his evil ways, renounced his bad habits, joined himself to the church, became really pious, and suddenly died of apoplexy only a month after he had become religious."

"That was surely better than if he had died before becoming so.   I don't think the change for the better, in his character, produced the change in his body for the worse ; or that the danger to his life was the consequence of the improvement in his morals.

It may be that certain changes in his physical condition, of which he was better conscious than anybody else, brought about the change of heart within him; and, fortunately for him, brought it about soon enough for his spiritual safety. I don't see why you should infer anything unfavourable to Major Bulmer's health, in consequence of the improved feeling which he shows towards us."

" I don't know, my child; there's no telling. It's all a mystery ; but I have my fears. I'm dubious that he is not altogether so sound of body after that accident."

" Why, mother, he walks as erect as ever."

" Oh ! that's owing to his pride. These Bulmers were always so. My poor brother used to say that if they were dying, they'd still carry their heads up, and would draw on their boots and put on their spurs as for a journey. But, what's to be done, my child, about these invitations ?"

" Oh ! we must accept them, mamma, as a matter of course."

" I don't see that, Paula."

" Surely, mamma, if Major Bulmer makes the first advances to reconciliation, you are not going to show a less Christian spirit than he."

" There is something in that, my dear, but—"

" Let the *but* alone, mamma. It properly belongs to the Bull family."

The old lady laughed.

" So it does, my child, so it does; that is very well said ;— but—"

" Again, mamma ! Now let me give you a sufficient reason for acceptance. You would not have me go alone; and I must be there, you know, as the whole neighbourhood will be present, and you would not have it appear that I was slighted, or that I had shown myself too little of a Christian to accept the overtures of a family between which and ours so long a feud has existed. You must accept the invitation, and go for my sake."

" Well, my dear, for *your* sake !" replied the indulgent dame, concealing, under the expression of her desire to gratify the damsel's wishes, some hankering tastes and curiosity of her own. The great object had thus been, safely and easily attained when Miss Bulmer made her appearance, and by some ill-judged, though very benevolent attempts to argue Madame Agnes-Theresa into the consent already won, had nearly driven the vessel out to sea again; like certain politicians of our acquaintance, who mar the pleasant progress of their own objects, by the too great passion for listening to their own eloquence. Many a good measure has been defeated in legislative assemblies, by a pert speech and an amiable epistle : both possessing more wind than wisdom. Our lady politician was of this unlucky brood, and, but for certain looks, nods, winks, and other sly proceedings—to say nothing of an absolute nudge or two—administered by pretty Paula, the ragoût of compliance, to use an oriental form of speech, would have certainly been spoiled in the cooking. But Miss Bulmer was fortunately silenced at the most dangerous crisis of the affair, and was persuaded to listen quite long enough to learn that grand-mamma had already consented, in regard to the especial wishes of the damsel, to attend the Golden Christmas at Bulmer Barony—the importance of the event seeming to justify the concession—it being the hundredth year since Christmas was celebrated in the same family and household. You may see on the gables of the house, in huge iron figures 1–7–5–1 ! It was the Golden Year in the history of the ancient fabric—ancient for the civilization of our country—which promises to attain the decrepitude of age, without realizing any of the famous dust and dignity of the antique. Though not exactly a favourite with Madame Girardin, our excellent maiden sister was not by any means the object of such dislike as had hitherto been felt for her brother by the former ; and the first business over, that of the invitation, the parties had a long domestic and parish chat together, which brought them still nearer in social respects. Of course, the two more ancient ladies looked together at the pigs and poultry, and—a matter of equal unctuousness in the sight of both—the best way of dressing and curing sausages, occupied an interesting half-hour to itself. You will at length suppose the interview over, and the maiden sister departed.

"Well, really," quoth Madame Girardin, "it shows that the good folks of the 'Barony' are coming to their senses at last. I do not see, my child, after the solicitude they have shown, how I could possibly escape this visit; and then, my dear, it's on your account too, you must remember."

" Certainly, mamma," returned the artful little puss, " you have always been good to me ! You know, *mamma*, you have to yield to my wishes."

And she wrapt her fairy-like arms about the neck of the venerable Hecate, and kissed her as fondly as you or I would have done the most rose-lipped virgin in the world.

But kissing is not now our cue—

> " This is no world
> To play with mammets, and to tilt with lips."

We have other and very different games on hand. I am signalled for the Wallet and the Strawberry Clubs—both hunting Societies—and both occurring the same week. Everybody knows, of course, that the clubs of the gentry exist in all our parishes, the hunters assembling weekly or semi-monthly, hunting the better part of the day, dining together at the Club House, or at some central point in the neighbourhood. The *wallet* club, by its name, shows the process for providing the dinner. Each hunter carries his wallet stored with creature comforts and a doomed bottle. The Major and myself were parties to both hunts, but neither of us succeeded, on these occasions, in getting a shot. We spent a merry day, however, with the good fellows of the parish. But we had another sport in reserve, of rather different character, to

10*

which a large party was invited; the affair to come off two
days before Christmas. You are aware that, in the larger
swamp and forest ranges of our low country, where population is
sparse, the hog runs absolutely wild. He is hunted up as the
season approaches when it is necessary to fatten him for the sham-
bles. Sometimes hogs will escape all notice for years. Turned
into the range after being marked, they flourish, or famish, on the
mast, just as the seasons decree. Sometimes they will show
themselves sluggishly fat, lying on sunny days of the winter in
heaps of half-rotted pine straw, enjoying themselves in the fashion
of Diogenes—asking nothing from man or fate but the small
amount of sunshine which reaches their repose through the tops
of two or three grouped pines or gums. The acorns are plenty.
They have fed fat that season, and are gruntingly good natured,
and growlingly sedate. You may walk over them and into them,
without irritating their self-esteem; almost without disturbing their
slumbers. But the case is otherwise in seasons when the mast
fails. Then they are gaunt and wolfish. Then they growl savagely, and you must not tread wantonly upon their sensibilities.
They drowse no longer in the sunshine than they can help. The
goad of necessity is ever at their flanks. They hear perpetually in
their ears the voice of a beastly fate which cries, "Root pig or die!"
and as they hear, each lank and angular porker thrusts his long
snout into the earth, and stirs the fields, from which the planter
has reaped, more thoroughly than the plough-share. The potato
fields, the ground-nut patch, are thus burrowed into, and the mea-
gre supplies, thus gleaned after the progress of the farmer, suffice for a while, not to fatten the animal, but to keep him alive.—
Even these fail, in season, and the farmer then, through rare benevolence, sends forth his grazier, who, with a daily sack of corn,
apportions to each, a small allowance, upon which he consents to
live a little longer. In this condition, the neglected hogs, grown
larger, and given to wandering through extensive and almost im-

penetrable recesses of swamp and thicket, become very wild and savage. They turn readily upon the dogs, and it requires a very vigorous cur, indeed, and a very bold one, to take them by the throat. They will sometimes give fierce battle to the hunter even, on horseback, and have been known to inflict serious if not fatal wounds upon the horse; while the rider, himself, must be wary enough in the encounter if he would escape from hurt. The long white tusks of an angry boar, which has never been honoured by the annual tribute of the barn, or mollified by the pickings of the farm-yard, are no trifling implements of battle, rashing short and sudden, against the thighs or ribs of the heedless hunters.

It was with no small pleasure that Major Bulmer was advised a week or so before Christmas, by his overseer, that he had found out the hiding place, in a neighbouring swamp, of a gang of "wild hogs" having his brand. Two of them were described as boars of the largest size and fiercest character. The Major instantly conceived the idea of a boar-hunt. It was his pride to emulate as much as possible, the character of the ancient English, and to practice those sports, the neglect of which, he insisted, were the first signs of the degeneracy of the age. The introduction recently, into the parish, of the jousts and tiltings of the knights of the middle ages,—as hath been well recorded by the antiquarian chronicler of the Charleston Courier,—served, perhaps, to suggest the present enterprise particularly to his mind. And the fact that the Boar's Head constituted, in old times, the preeminent dish at every feudal English table on Christmas day, made him resolve that this grim trophy should also adorn his own, on the approaching anniversary. To some six or eight of the young knights who had distinguished themselves at the last tournament, proper notice was given, and, at the time appointed, we had the pleasure of seeing them assemble, each armed with a boar spear and *couteau de chasse.* There were the Knights of St. John, and of Santee ; Knights of the Rose and of the Dragon ; Knights of the Bleeding Heart, and of the Swan ; and others, whom I need not name. I confess to figuring as the Knight of Keawah,—the old Indian name of Ashley River,—while a young friend, from the city also, came up in season to enact the part of the Knight of Etiwan— or of Cooper River. It was a proper day which we took for the sport,—dry, and a mellow sunshine in the heavens and upon the earth. We rode under the guidance of the overseer, and under the lead of the Knight of the Dragon,—the Major being still a little too sore and stiff to head the party, though nothing short of a broken limb could have kept him from partaking of the adventure. We took with us but five dogs, but these were of known blood and courage. These were Clench, Gripe, Wolf, Bull, and Belcher. It happened, though we did not know it when we set out, that we were followed by another,—a stranger,—which nobody knew,—a gaunt, gray beagle, of very long body, and a modest, rather sneaking deportment. He had not waited for enlistment, received no bounty, and, seeking only the honour of the thing, went as an obscure volunteer. We never noticed his appearance until we were in the thick of the fight.

The dogs knew very well what we were after. One of them, following the overseer, had tracked the prey before. We had, however, some trouble and a long ride to find them, as they had changed their hiding places repeatedly since the day of their discovery. The dogs scattered in the search. They had penetrated a great mucky bog, at several points, while the hunters skirted it, waiting for the signal. An occasional yelp, or bark, would at times excite us, but, for a while, we were disappointed. At length, one of the dogs gave tongue, shortly and quickly, and with evident anger in his tone. The hunter is apt to know his dogs by their voices. The Major said,—

" That's Belcher,—a sure dog,—better to report truly than to fight fiercely. Let's put in."

With the words, we spurred forward in the direction of the sounds, making but slow headway through the thick matted copse and underbrush which covered the entrance. But we got through at last, and found ourselves in a wood, where the trees were of considerable size, standing sufficiently open,—gum, water-oak, and pine,—with occasional patches of gall bushes, and dense masses, here and there, of cane, bramble and shrubs, with thin flats of water lying between, and leaving little tussocky beds, high and dry, on which we found frequent but abandoned beds of the beasts we were in search of. We rode forward now at a trot, Belcher, the dog giving tongue more rapidly, and, being now joined by another dog, whose bark was less frequent, but very fierce; and one which the Major did not recognize;—a fact which somewhat worried him. Soon, we saw the overseer, with two other dogs, approaching from a point on our right; and, as we were joining, the form of the absent dog, Gripe, came rushing by us from the rear, and making for the scene of clamour, which appeared to rise from a recess in the wood still beyond us. This we could attain only by passing through another dense skirt of undergrowth, vines, shrubs, canes and gall bushes. Four dogs we had just marked as they passed, yet we had heard two tongues within the covert. We had no time to speculate upon the surplus 'tongue'; the clamour was momently increasing. The enemy was evidently brought to bay. Poising our boar spears aloft, we forced our way through the copse, at the expense of some scratched faces, torn skirts, and caps lost for the moment. Breaking into the opening, the whole scene was apparent at a glance, and in one of those very spots where, our object being to see and to engage in the *meleé*, we should have chosen it to occur. There was a spectacle indeed. There were three hogs of immense size, of the breed, called, I think, the ' Irish Grazier.' They were long bodied animals, with long legs, grisly and angular in aspect and outline, and all with ominous tusks. There was a huge sow, very thin, with some eight or ten pigs. There were

besides, two or three good sized shoats. A single boar, and he, the
largest, seemed to be in good condition. He was evidently one
of those fierce, insolent and powerful beasts, who are known to
plant their shoulders against a worm fence, and by main force to
shove it over. These were all grouped together, the pigs within
the circle, so as to present a front on every hand, when we came
in sight. The dogs had surrounded them, but kept at a decent
distance. They became more adventurous the moment we appeared, and dashed gallantly in among the herd. But it was a
word and a blow only ; the sharp bark was followed by a sharper
cry, and we could see the blood-stains instantly upon the shoulders of one limping beast, and the gash along the ribs of another,
who howled himself out of the fight, only to sink down, seemingly
fainting in the water.

" Bull has got his quietus, I'm afraid," quoth the Major, poising
his spear, and preparing for a charge.

" Stop, Major," quoth the Knight of the Dragon ; " let's have
fair play. It will not be easy to have a chance, or to work successfully, while they keep herded in that hollow square. We must
try and seperate them. If you will suffer me, I will but prick one
or more of the beasts with my spear, and allow the dogs to break
into their ranks. At all events, suffer me to try it."

The Major held up somewhat unwillingly, and the young Knight
darted forward gallantly, brought up his steed, which was equally
fiery and shy, with a sharp thrust, into both flanks, of a Spanish
rowell, and, rising in his stirrups, dexterously passed the broad iron
spear along the shoulder and sides of one of the largest boars.
The savage beast in a moment snapped at the assailing instrument,
but fortunately took hold of the part only where it was sheathed
with iron. He shook himself free from it a moment after, and as
it was withdrawn instantly, he wheeled about in the direction
of his assailant, who had now ridden past. This changed his attitude, exposing his broad flank to the Major, whom nothing now

could keep from the charge. He made it with commendable spirit, and drove his spear clean through the neck of the boar. The wounded beast, with an angry cry, turned suddenly before the shaft could be withdrawn, and the iron head was broken off in the wound. The suffering must have been extreme, for he wildly dashed at the steed of his assailant, which backed suddenly against a cypress, reared, plunged and dashed forwards, almost into the circle where the other hogs were still collected; and, but that the Major was a famous horseman, he would have been unseated. The wounded boar was not, however, permitted to carry the affair after his own fashion. The Knight of Santee came to the Major's rescue, and adroitly drove his iron in between the gnashing teeth of the brute, piercing obliquely through the neck again, and compelling another cry, between a grunt and a roar. The blood gushed freely from the wounds, and the scent of it had the usual stimulating effect upon the dogs. The first in was the gaunt gray, of whom nobody knew anything,—the volunteer in the expedition. He had the boar by the nose in a moment. A single toss and twist threw the monster down, and, leaping from his horse, the Knight of the Dragon passed his keen *couteau de chasse* over his weasand.

The other parties, hogs, dogs, and knights, were by no means idle during this progress. The operations of the Major, by which one of the grimmest of the boars had been withdrawn from the circle, left it penetrable. The dogs dashed in once more. The pigs squealed, the sow gave battle fiercely, but was taken by the snout, by the dog Gripe, and turned over in a jiffy; the overseer, jumping down and tying her with certain buckskin thongs, with which he had come properly provided. The capture of the pigs continued to employ him during the rest of the affair. For this, we had a fair field; and, by the way, the noblest quarry. The Knight of the Dragon, like a courteous gentleman, kept aloof, leaving the sport to those who had taken no hand in the killing of the first boar. Major Bulmer was disarmed, by the breaking of his spear, and looked on with rare impatience, while the conflict continued. It was not allowed, be it remembered, to use any other weapons than spear and knife. There had been little sport, and none of the classical, in the affair, but for this restriction. The two remaining boars confronted us, with their little, round, sharp, malignant eyes, telling us, as well as words could do, what we might expect from their monstrous white tusks, which stuck out three goodly inches or more from either jaw. To seperate these two, to divide our forces against them, and to begin the attack, were all matters of very brief arrangement. To the Knights of St. John, the Bleeding Heart, and myself, were assigned the conquest of the largest of the grim graziers. The second named dashed forward valiantly, and delivered his spear, well addressed, fairly at the throat of the brute; but, turning suddenly, at the moment—not disposed to wait for the assault—he made at the horse of the attacking knight, who barely recovered himself in season to wheel about and escape the glaring tusks that almost caught the courser's sides. Following up his onslaught, I put in, successfully taking the fierce brute just behind the ear and below the junction of the head and neck. The spear passed in,—a severe thrust,—which was only arrested by the skull. I was fortunate in drawing forth the weapon before he could turn about, and seize upon it, as he strove to do. At this moment, no aspect could be more full of rage and fury than that which the boar presented. His back was absolutely curved like a bow, the bristles were raised, erect, and standing out in points like those of the porcupine; his eyes seemed to flash a grey, malignant light, like so much white heat, while the bristling brows, long and wiry, stood out straight. The teeth and tusks were bare; and, standing, regarding us with a sidelong watchfulness, there was a mixture of rage and subtlety in the look of the boar, that showed him no merciful customer, could he ever make himself fairly felt. That he had the fullest purpose to do so, every raised and corded muscle of his body seemed to declare.

It was a point of honour to give the Knight of St. John a chance, so I held my spear uplifted, and suffered him to ride up to the charge. To say that the Cavalier in question is one of the best riders in the country, one of the best exercised in the lance, and can ride at a ring with a grace to charm the most fastidious of the damsels of the parish, would be mere surplusage. To see him, with his beaver up,—by which I mean his fur cap, with patent leather peak,—his enormous mass of sable whiskers, and elaborately twirled mustache,—to behold him rising in the stirrup and levelling the spear,—then, as he drives the spur into the sides of the courser, to see him lance the direct shaft into the throat of the beast, a seemingly mortal thrust—would have given a grim delight to any ancient Nimrod of the German forests. One would have supposed such a thrust, so well delivered, with so much equal address and force, quite enough to have settled the accounts in full of the victim; but not so! It seemed to act only as a new spur to his fury. He dashed headlong at the horse of his assailant— which curved with a sweep handsomely out of his way—then, with a strange caprice, dashed on the opposite side, just as the Knight of the Bleeding Heart was slowly approaching, lance uplifted, and never dreaming of his enjoying another chance at the grim enemy. He was taken completely by surprise, and, before he could anticipate the danger, or wheel out of the way, the sharp, white, felonious tusk of the boar rashed against the foreshoulder of his beast, swift and deep, so that you could hear the griding of the keen instrument against the bone. With a terrible snort of fear, his mane rising and ears backing, the horse dashed wildly off, at an acute angle, turning as if upon a well oiled pivot, working under electricity; and, in the twinkling of a musquito's wing, the handsome young Knight of the Bleeding Heart, might be seen describing a short evolution in the air, vulgarly called the summerset— supposed to be only a vulgar contraction for "some upset," or "some overset,"—and falling incontinently into the midst of the

11

conflict going on just then, between the remaining boar and the Knights of Etiwan, the Rose, and the Swan. Out of one peril into another, the Knight of the Bleeding Heart seemed in danger of literally verifying his claim to the title. Of a certainty, that of the Broken Head, seemed absolutely unavoidable. Nor was this the only danger; for, at the precise moment when he fell into the midst of the striving parties, the spears of the Knights of Etiwan and the Rose, had actually crossed in the throat of the boar, and he was gnashing, and rashing, and dashing, on both sides alternately, keeping up a sort of see-saw motion, the crossed spears maintaining for him the balance admirably, and the two knights, during his phrensied movements, finding it difficult to withdraw their weapons from his tough side. You have heard of the little Canadian hunter, who was pitched by his horse among a herd of galloping buffaloes, and straddled the great bull, and was horsed from him to the back of the great cow, then precipitated among and over and between and through and above, a forest of little calves! Such, on a minor scale, was the sort of progress made by our Knight of the Bleeding Heart—first over the great boar, then flirted off upon the sow—who lay prostrate and tied—then rolling from her embrace among the swarm of little piggies, who were grouped around her, ten in number, each with nose to the ground, and tail curling in the air. He was thus tossed about, with a most feathery facility, for a moment, settling down finally like a stone, in very close proximity to the sow. Their groans were so mingled, that it was not easy to distinguish between them; and, confounding them together for a moment, we almost apprehended that the Knight of the Bleeding Heart would soon be in want of an epitaph. Several of us dismounted and rushed to his assistance, Major Bulmer, in the meanwhile, eagerly rushing in to slit the jugular of the boar, who had succumbed to the Knight of Santee and myself; and the Knights of the Dragon and Swan doing the same good service for the third boar, with which he and the Knights of the Rose and Etiwan had been doing battle. We picked up the champion of the Bleeding Heart, and found him with bleeding nostrils. This was his worst injury. He was stunned and considerably scratched, but, alighting just upon the boar's back, tilted next upon the sow's, and, rolling over finally among the pigs, the shock of his fall was measurably broken. It might have been otherwise a fatal one ; for he was slung from the saddle, headlong, like a stone. It was surprising, too, that he should have been thus unhorsed, for he ranked as a first rate rider. But he was taken by surprise, and the lack of vigilance is usually the wreck of skill. The worst of his misfortune is to come. That he should have suffered so *little* was the evil feature in his case. Had leg, or arm, or neck, been broken, the mishap would have risen into tragic dignity. As it resulted, it was simply ludicrous, and the Knight of the Bleeding Heart was every where laughed at as the Knight of the Bloody Nose!

CHAPTER XV.

A FLARE UP BETWEEN MOTHER AND DAUGHTER.

We bagged our prey as well as we could. The overseer had providently ordered a cart to follow the party, and our spoils filled it :—the dead hogs being at the bottom, while the maternal porker, still unhurt, with her numerous progeny, grunted all the way home, from a spacious but bloody couch in the centre of her slain associates. I forbear numerous small details of our adventure, satisfied to have given all the material facts. I may mention here, that, subsequently, one of the party, who possessed a wonderful faculty for caricature, executed a drawing to the life, and brimfull of spirit, of the *serio-ludicro* exhibition of the Knight of the Bleeding Heart, at the moment of his unexpected descent among the swine. He is bestraddling the mammoth boar, on all fours, hands thrown forward, as if grasping at the tail of the beast, while his legs are scattered 'all abroad' over the animal's neck. The rest of the hogs are grouped around in various attitudes, more or less influenced by the advent of the Knight. The little pigs, in particular, with snouts uplifted and tails upcurled, are recoiling with evident awe and apprehension, seeming to ask,—'Heavens! what are we to look for next?' The picture is preserved with great care at the Bulmer Barony, where it may be seen at any moment,* much to the secret disquiet of the graceful young Knight, who is the hero of the scene.

But I must not linger in the narration of such episodes, even though they constituted the chief exercises and amusements of the Christmas holidays. Day and night, for two weeks, we were on the move,—now to this club house, or that,—this or that dance or dinner party,—seeing new faces daily with the old ones, and having no moment unemployed with brisk and pleasant exercises. I must not forget to mention that, in the meanwhile, Ned Bulmer grew better, and, as his sorenesses of body lessened, those of his heart seemed to increased. As soon as he was able to go forth, we went together on a visit to Bonneau Place, where he had the felicity of enjoying a more civil welcome from the grandmother than he had altogether expected, and where I succeeded, by going out with that excellent old lady to admire her poultry, in giving him a chance for a half hour's sweet secret chat with Paula. Of course, nobody cares to listen to the prattle of young lovers, who are mere children always, the sympathies and affections leaving them no motive for the exercise of thoughts.

Leaving it to the reader's imagination and experience, to supply this portion of my chapter, let me peep, for a while, into the habitation of my own cynosure. We will suppose ourselves, therefore,

---

*This was true at the moment of the writing; but, in a note just received from Mr. Cooper, he tells me that the picture has disappeared, no body knows how, feloniously cut out of its frame, while it hung in the passage way; Major Bulmer being inclined to think that the deed was done, either by the young Knight or some of the Porker family, they being the only parties interested in destroying the proofs of such an adventure.—EDITOR.

at Mazyck Place, on the morning of the day when Madame Girardin and Paula received their invitations to the grand festival to come off on Christmas, at the Barony.   Mrs. Mazyck and Beatrice had received invitations at the same time, and they, too, required to sit in council upon the matter.   The subject was one of great doubt and deliberation in the one household as in the other.   Most people of insular life, living in the country, and only occasionally in society, are tenacious and jealous of their social claims in much greater degree than people of a city.   Seclusion is a great nurse of self-esteem, and all matters, however minute and unimportant, which affect the social position or estimates, are weighed with a nicety and observance, in rural life, which really provoke a smile only among persons to whom the jostle with humanity is a daily and constantly recurring thing.   In the city, the crowd is always compensative for the ill-treatment of the clique.   You care little for that denial or neglect from the one group, which is more than made up to you by the attentions of another.   You find refuge in one set from the exclusiveness of its rival; and, where the city is a large one, there is no class or street, without a sufficiently solacing circle, in which you may find wit, intelligence, grace of manner, and virtue, quite adequate, at once, to your claims and your desires. Accordingly, you miss no consideration, and are comparatively heedless of neglect.   People, tacitly, make their communities on every side, and he must be a poor devil, indeed, who may not readily find all the companionship which suits his tastes and necessities.   But, the case is far otherwise in the sparsely settled abodes of our interior; and this is just in degree with the real wealth and resources of the planters.   Large plantations push away permanent society, and make it inconvenient to procure it regularly.   Hence, the hospitality of all those regions which continually welcome their guests from abroad.   Hence, again, a sort of rivalry among the several proprietors in the state which they keep and the entertainment of their guests.   But this aside.   Enough here to indicate the sort of

11*

influence which helps to make people tenacious of every claim or right, and resentful of the most shadowy appearance of neglect or slight. The self-esteem which is continually nursed, while it is the parent of a character which delights in noble exhibitions and revolts at meannesses, is yet apt to be watchful, jealous, suspicious, and forever on the *qui vive* to let you understand that it feels itself quite as good as its neighbour; that it is quite independent of the social sunshine issuing from your portals; that it has friends enough, and fortune enough, and guests enough, all of its own, and no thanks to any body,—*et cetera, et cetera, et cetera!*

Mrs. Mazyck was a proud and stately lady, of real worth, of excellent habits and family, some wealth, and great hospitality. But she was touched with this very infirmity of self-esteem, and jealous self-esteem, in considerable degree. She noted your absences, the infrequency of your calls, your failure in solicitude, your want of reverence when present. She seemed to keep a calendar, in which all things were regularly set down against your account. She would receive no excuses,—she had no faith in apologies,— took nothing into consideration,—made no allowances,—when these charges were once entered on her books. You had been sick perhaps,—"Hum! Yes! so I hear, but he could find health enough to call on Mrs. G—— or Mrs. B——." You had been very much employed in settling the affairs of the estate, had been to the city, and had really been too busy to make any visits.— "Perhaps! Yet it is something curious that business could not keep him away from the party at Mrs. ——'s." True: but that was a family rëunion, and you went by special invitation. "Oh! I don't need to be told of the difference between a lively party, a dance and a supper, and the dull duty of calling to see a tedious old woman." So, you must beware, when actually within the charmed circle of her presence, that you linger not too long beside any other dame, whose state or position is at all comparable to her own;—so, beware also, that, when making your respects to her, you betray not too much eagerness to cross the room to listen to the gay chat of the P's, or G's, or B's, or S's. You will be remembered for all these offences against her *amour propre*. The haughty lady will as indifferently detach you from her hooks of favour, and cast you out into the stream, as the angler casts off the worm, that, having suffered the infliction of frequent nibblings, is no longer able or willing to wriggle upon the hook.

Behold her, as she sits, grave, dignified and stern, beside the fire place, stately in her purple-cushioned and luxurious rocker, in that trim, well-furnished parlour, great mirrors lining the lofty walls, and rich curtains of blue and white, trimmed with silver, subduing still more the feeble light of the December sun, as it glides, like an unnoticed angel, into the apartment. The old lady has evidently clad herself that morning in her ancientest social buckram. Her toilet, as usual, has been elaborately made;—and her black velvet, flowing and abundant, is as smooth as the daily goings on of her household. Her tiring woman has dressed her hair with more than her wonted nicety; and the few curls which nature has left to her, or which,—making a certain feminine sacrifice to worldly notions,—she has allotted to herself, are admirably balanced on each side of her high forehead. Her movements are quite too measured to suffer her to decompose them throughout the whole day. There they will keep their place till folded out of sight for the night, either beneath her night-cap, or in the nice little antique rose-wood cabinet of her *boudoir*. She belongs to an old school, in which state and form are habitual, and where, if any thing fails, it is nature only, and that art which is its proper shadow,—which is modestly content and happy when suffered to be its handmaid.

The good lady meditates bolt upright. A work table is beside her, on which rests a gold-edged, pink-hued billet, the contents partly legible to her eye where it lies. She takes it up, scans it over, lays it down, and uplifts her eyebrows. Her lips, you see, are closely compressed. The effect is not a pleasant one on an antique visage, particularly where the lips are thin. She again takes up the billet, but as she hears a voice and a footstep, she again lays it upon the table, this time with a little hurry in her manner. She evidently does not desire to be seen meditating its contents.

Beatrice enters, calm, sweet, as if all her passions were subdued to angels. Beatrice possesses real dignity,—a quality that is free from any ostentatious consciousness of its possession. She has no affectations of any kind. No temper could be more serene,—no sunshine more agreeable in its warmth, or less broken by the interposing shadows of vanity, or arrogance, or pretence, or presumption. But I will let Beatrice,—my Beatrice,—reveal herself. I will not undertake to describe her, for I should never know where to begin, or where to stop. Beatrice quietly approaches her mother, and takes up the billet.

" Sould this not be answered to-day, mother ?"

" What is it, my child ?" was the answer of mamma, profoundly ignorant of the nature of the note.

" The invitation of Major Bulmer for Christmas !"

" Oh !—ah !—and what answer do you propose to send, Beatrice ?"

" What answer, mother ? We accept, of course !"

" I don't see why of course."

The damsel looked her surprise. The mother proceeded.

" I am not sure that I shall accept."

" Indeed ! Why not ?"

" You are at liberty to do as you please. You are young, and will like to be among the young people ; but, as it is quite as much on your account as my own, that I shall decline going to Major Bulmer, you, too, perhaps, may see the propriety of following my example."

" On my account."

" Yes, my child, on your account partly, and partly on my own."

" Why, mother, this is very strange."

" You may think so. Young people are very unobservant, and the young people of the present generation, I must say, are quite too indifferent to the sort of treatment they receive. They love society too much; they are ever ready to take it on any terms. Now, for my part, *I* have always been taught to receive it as a due, and not as a favour, and to welcome it as a right rather than a benevolence."

Beatrice had witnessed quite too many instances of this sort of crotchettiness on the part of her excellent mamma, not to see, at once, that her soup had been temporarily under seasoned. She had acquired some skill in the business of soothing the irritated appetite, and supplying the ingredients necessary,—to use an orientalism,—for the conserve of a delicious temper. But she was really taken by surprise at this demonstration in the present quarter. She had seen the Major and her mamma exceedingly intimate only a week or two before. Nay, she had seen sufficient proofs, by which she had been greatly disquieted, of the secret object which the two parties had equally meditated of bringing Ned Bulmer and herself together. What had brought about the present alteration in the state of affairs? What had cooled off the parties? Beatrice was not unwilling, I may say in this place, that there should be an end to the conspiracy against her happiness and that of Ned. But she had no desire that there should be a cloud and a wall between the two families. She was worried accordingly. Mammas, she well knew, having single,—ought I not rather to say only,—daughters, are apt to be fussy and fidgetty; just as you see an old hen, whom the hawk has robbed of every chicken but one,—making more clack and clutter, and showing more pride and pother, than all the poultry yard beside;—and the dear girl had long since resolved, that she, at least, would not contribute in any way to make herself the chicken so ridiculously conspicuous. There was no more unpresuming, unpretending damsel, for one of her pretensions, in the world. Now, as the last sentence of her mamma was tingling in her ears, she fancied she could catch the clues of her difficulty; but her guess did not persuade her to spare the excellent old lady any portion of the necessity of speaking out, in proper terms, the subject of her embarrassment.

"Really, mamma, you speak in oracles. I can't conceive why you should speak of society accorded to you as a benevolence rather than as a due,—and that, too, on the part of the Bulmer family. They seem to me to have always distinguished you with the most becoming attentions. Miss Janet is one of the most docile and humble creatures in the world, and she has been solicitously heedful of us both ; the old Major, himself, has been so attentive, particularly of late, that, really, mamma, I had begun to entertain some apprehensions that the Fates were about to punish me with a step-father, in order to make me atone for some of my offences."

"Beatrice,—Miss Mazyck,"—with a most freezing aspect of rebuke,—the old lady drawing up her knees and laying her hands solemnly in her lap,—" You know not what you are saying."

"Oh! yes, mamma, I know very well. How else could I account for the long letter you received from the Major last summer, and the long letter you wrote to him in return, neither of which did you suffer me to see, though you do me the honour usually to make me your amanuensis with all your other correspondents."

"There were reasons for the exception, Miss Mazyck."

"Precisely, mamma; that's what I'm saying,—there was a special reason for that exception ————"

"I said *reasons*, not a *special* reason, Miss Mazyck."

"Well, mamma, and I thought it only reasonable to conclude your reasons to be resolvable into a special reason. When, after our return, the Major was the first to call upon you, and when you took him out, under the pretext of visiting the loom-house, and the smoke-house, and the poultry-yard, and heaven knows what else ; and when you were gone together almost an hour,— how could I suppose any thing else, than the particular danger to myself, if not to you, that I have mentioned ?"

" You are disrespectful, Beatrice."

" Surely not, mamma."

" You know not what you are saying. You know not the business on which Major Bulmer wrote me that letter and paid me that visit."

" Certainly not, mamma, I only conjectured, and I give you my conjecture. As you never condescended to let me into the secret, I naturally thought that it more particularly concerned yourself."

" You are a very foolish child, Beatrice. The letters concerned you, rather than me. The visit was paid on your account. If I went out with Major Bulmer, *you* were left here *with his son.*"

" No, mamma, you mistake ; I was left with Mr. Cooper."

" Yes, Miss Mazyck, and that reminds me of the first show of disrespect, to our family, on the part of Major Bulmer's. Mr. Edward Bulmer treated you with so little consideration, that he left you as soon as our backs were turned, and, when found, was stretched off and sleeping in the library. Was that proper treatment of my daughter ?"

" Really, mamma, I never missed him."

The old lady gave her daughter a severe and suspicious glance, but did not answer the remark. She proceeded thus :

" Whether you *missed* him or not, does not alter the fact with regard to his conduct on that occasion. It was highly improper, and very disrespectful. But his disrespect did not end here. On the night of the party, he did not dance with you once."

" In that, if there be any thing to blame, I am the offender. He applied to me twice or three times for the privilege of dancing with me, and each time I was engaged."

" Yes, but could he not have engaged you for the dance afterwards ?"

" I am not sure but he sought to do so. It is certain, that, throughout the evening, I was engaged, most usually, one or more dances ahead."

" If there had been a will for it, Beatrice, there had been a way."

" That is, if both our wills agreed. There, I conceive, the difficulty to have lain. I confess, I see nothing in Mr. Bulmer's conduct, on that occasion, which could be construed into slight or disrespect."

" You do not want to see, Beatrice."

" You are right, mamma. I am not anxious, at any time, to pick
out and seek for the flaws and infirmities in my neighbour."

" That may be a very pious principle of conduct, my daughter,
which, in every day matters, I cannot disapprove of; but there are
cases where a proper pride requires the exercise of proper resent-
ment. The conduct of Major Bulmer and his son, has not satisfied
me *since* the night of the ball. They have neither of them dark-
ened these doors since."

" Why, mother, how could they? You surely could not expect
them, suffering, as they did, from such an accident that night.
Mr. Edward Bulmer has been laid up with a broken arm, and the
old Major was covered with bruises."

" But he could find his limbs and body sound enough to visit
Mrs. Girardin."

" Surely, and he was bound to do so; the friendly care, the
charitable kindness, the magnanimity of the old lady, that night,
in giving her assistance, so promptly, and with so much real benevolence and kindness to the sufferers, called for the earliest and
most grateful acknowledgment. As a gentleman, merely, if not
as a Christian and human being, Major Bulmer could do no less
than pay her a visit, of thanks and gratitude, as soon as he was
able."

" Yes, and Miss Bulmer could go too. Both could pay their
respects in that quarter, and neither in ours."

" Ah! mamma! so you find cause of complaint in poor Miss
Janet, too, one of the best of human creatures."

" Yes, indeed; if they could visit one house, they might well
visit another; and there were reasons why they should have been
here, if only to explain."

" Explain !"

" Yes, explain ! You can't, at present, understand ; but I mean it when I say explain ! There's another thing, Beatrice. Mrs. Girardin and Paula Bonneau have both been invited to the Christmas party at Major Bulmer's. I have it from Sally, the cook. Her husband, Ben, belonging to Paula, told Sally of the invitation, and of the very day when it was given."

" What more natural. The Major and Miss Bulmer could not surely have omitted them." .

" What! after the long quarrel between the families ?"

" For that very reason, mother. A quarrel is not to be kept up for ever in a Christian country ; and what better occasion for reconciliation than when one of the parties assists the other in a case of extremity ; and what better season than this, when God himself despatches his only Son on a mission of Love, Forgiveness, and final reconciliation between himself and his offending people ? Really, mamma, if you were to say to others what you have said to me, people would begin to suspect you of Paganism."

" Better call me a Pagan, at once, Miss Mazyck !" growled mamma, gathering herself up in the attitude of one about to spring. " But, it is not that Mrs. Girardin and her grand-daughter have been invited, that I complain. But when I know that the invitation was sent to *them*, a whole day and night before any was sent to us, *that*, Miss Mazyck ———"

" That, mamma, is one of those offences that cannot but be committed, and which there is no helping. It is done every day. All cannot be served at the same moment. While one's soup is scalding him, another, at the extremity of the table, finds his a little cooler than soup ought to be. Somebody must always be last."

" But I am not pleased to be that somebody, Miss Mazyck."

" And, in this case, mamma, I am very sure you are not. I would wager something that if Mrs. Girardin received the first, you had the second invitation."

12

"Perhaps; but that does not altogether satisfy me, considering the terms on which Major Bulmer and myself stood together."

"Ah! those terms, mamma," said Beatrice archly and with a smile. The mother did not attend to the remark, but proceeded as if she had not heard it:

"But, I see the whole secret. The fact is, that Mrs. Girardin has a good deal of foresight and a grand-daughter, and Major Bulmer has a handsome fortune and a son; and charity by the wayside, may bring its benefits into the parlour; and they do say that Miss Paula is not insensible to the wealth and person of Mr. Edward Bulmer, and so ———"

"Mother, mother!" cried Beatrice reproachfully; "do not suffer yourself to speak such things. Mrs. Girardin, I am sure, would have done for the blind beggar, by the highway, all that she did for Major Bulmer ———"

"What! with her pride?"

"Her pride is ridiculous enough, I grant you, but so far as I have ever seen, it has never been indulged at the expense of her humanity. I am sure, at least, that her pride would have been enough to keep her from any calculations in respect to the Bulmer family, its son and wealth. She is certainly too proud for any scheming to obtain any thing from that or any other family. As for Paula Bonneau, I know no woman who better deserves the best favour of fortune in a husband; but she is to be sought, mother, and she will not herself be found on the search for a lover. Let me so far correct your opinion as to tell you what the world reports in respect to Paula Bonneau. It says that Edward Bulmer has long been her devoted, if not her accepted lover, and that she is truly attached to him, in spite of the hostility of her grandmother, so that most of your suspicions are wrong, if those of the world be right."

"It is impossible, Beatrice,—it is impossible!" said the mother, pushing away the stool beneath her feet, and rising with an air of outraged dignity. "The terms between Major Bulmer and myself———"

"Ah! *those terms* again, mother. Pray, what is the mysterious nature of this affair between you and Major Bulmer? Really, unless you tell me plainly the state of the case, I shall have to fall back upon my old suspicions. My powers of divination yield me no other conjectures."

The mother quickened her movements across the room, then wheeling about, confronted the daughter with a somewhat imperious manner, as she said,—

"Well, if you must know,—and, under present appearances, I see no reason to maintain a useless secrecy,—you must know that Major Bulmer has proposed for you, and that I consented ——"

"Major Bulmer, for me,—why, mamma, he is old enough for my grandfather!" cried the girl in unaffected astonishment.

"Pshaw, Beatrice, you surely know what I mean. He proposed far you on behalf of his son."

"And you consented?"

"Yes,—I consented. I thought the match a very eligible one."

"But how could you consent, mother, to any thing of the sort? Did you mean that I was to have no voice in the matter?"

"No, by no means; but I took it for granted, my daughter, that you would see the thing in its proper light,—see the advantages of such a match—and I consented that the Major should open the matter to his son ——"

"Heavens! mother! what have you done!" exclaimed Beatrice, the rich red suffusing cheeks and neck, while a singular brightness flashed freely out from her dilating eyes. It was her turn to rise and pace the apartment. "What have you done! How have you shamed me! So, Edward Bulmer is to be persuaded, under an arrangement with my own mother, to behold in me the proper handmaid upon whom it is only necessary that he should bestow his smiles, in order to obtain submission. I am to be made happy by the bounty of his love. Oh! mother! mother! how could you do this thing?"

"But, my dear, you see it in a very peculiar and improper light. I—"

" I see it in the only light. It appears by your own showing,—and, indeed, I *know* the fact,—that Mr. Bulmer has had no part in this beautiful arrangement. He must be argued into it; and his father must provide him with the proper spectacles—his or your's, mother,—looking through which, he is to discover what he never of himself could see, that I am the proper young woman whom he should espouse. You have done wrong, mother,—you have been guilty of a great cruelty. You have shamed me in my own eyes."

" How !—how !"

" Who will suppose,—Major Bulmer or his son, think you ?—that *you* would venture to pledge the affections of your daughter, to one whose affections have yet to be persuaded."

" Oh ! no ! by no means. I told the Major that you knew nothing——"

" Of course ! and had I known every thing, it still would have been an amiable maternal error—quite venial and rather pretty, perhaps—to have made exactly the same assurance. The Major believes just as much of it as he pleases,—the son as little ;—and I—and I—I am to appear as the humble virgin, dutiful at the threshold, as another Ruth, entreating to be taken into the household of the wealthy Boaz. Oh ! what have you done, mother ! What have you done !"

And a passion of tears followed the drawing of the humiliating picture. The mother was astounded, and began to fear that, in her previous consideration of the subject, she had excluded from view some of the proper lights for judging it. She began to falter, and to make assurances. But the daughter had risen in strength and dignity, just in degree as the mother had declined. Her tears had ceased to flow, but her soul was up in arms, and the fires now flowed from the eyes that lately wept. Her form, always lofty and noble, now rose into a sort of queenly majesty, that filled the old lady with admiration.

" As for Edward Bulmer," said Beatrice, " he is not for me, nor I for him. I have long known that he loved Paula Bonneau ;

and I have good reason to believe that his love is requited. But even had he been willing, mother, his father willing, and you willing, *I* should not have willed the connexion."

"But, Beatrice, my daughter," interposed the mother, now thoroughly alarmed, "you do not tell me you will marry against my consent."

"No mother; but I mean to tell you that I will never marry until I have my own consent!"

A carriage at this moment rolled into the court below. The mother looked through the blinds.

"It is Major Bulmer's, and Miss Janet is getting out."

"One word then, mother,—*we both* must accept this invitation, and it must be frankly and unreservedly—unless we wish the whole parish to suspect that, in the union of the houses of Bulmer and Bonneau, Beatrice Mazyck has suffered a mortification,—Beatrice Mazyck has been rejected by him to whom her mother has offered her in sacrifice."

"Oh! my child! How can you say so?"

The dialogue was interrupted by the entrance of the ancient but amiable maiden, whom Beatrice received with an affectionate kiss, and her mother with a laborious smile. It need not scarcely be said, that Beatrice had her own way, and that the invitation was accepted.

CHAPTER XVI.

CHRISTMAS EVE.

Time, meanwhile, had been hobbling forward, after the usual fashion, and with his wonted rapidity. He brings us at length to Christmas eve. But the old Egyptian don't find us unprepared. He does not catch us napping, though he may at the '*nappy*.'

12*

We have taken him by the forelock. We have been getting steam upon him for a goodly month or more. Major Bulmer has failed in none of his supplies; and aunt Janet has been doing the *crusty*, in spite of her proverbial sweetness of temper,—and because of it—in the pantry and bake-house, for a week of eleven days. What a wilderness of mince-pies have issued from her framing hands; what a forest of patties and petties, cocoanut and cranberry;—what deserts of island and trifle; what seas of jelly; what mountains of blanc mange. Eggs have grown miraculously scarce. There is a hubbub now going on between the fair spinster and her lordly brother.

"But, Janet, by Jove, this will never do! You mustn't stint us in Egg-nog. Better give up a bushel of your pudding stuff, than that we should have less than several bushels of eggs."

"But, brother, there will still be enough. You know the ladies seldom take egg-nog, now a days."

"I know no such thing, and don't believe it. We must provide enough, at all events. Send out Tom and Jerry; let them scour the country and pick up all they can. These women with their parties!"

"Was ever such a man as brother!" cried Miss Janet to me, with bare arms, uplift, and well sprinkled with flour. She had been kneading that her public should not need, which is certainly patriotism, if not Christian charity. But I have no time to listen to her, or to speculate upon her virtues. The Major summoned me forth to look at the hogs. Thirty were slaughtered last night. There they hang, the long-bodied, white porkers, thoroughly cleaned, like so many convicts, decently dressed for the first time in their lives, when about to pay the penalty of their offences. "Not a rogue among them," quoth the Major, "that weighs less than 250 nett." Yesterday, there was a beef shot. We must go and look at him, see him quartered, and estimate his weight and importance also. Huge tubs and wooden platters of sausage meat entreat our attention, and I assist Miss Janet in measuring out pepper, black and red, and sage and thyme, and salt and saltpetre, that the sausage meat may be as grateful to the taste as it is fully great to the eye. The Major and his sister are the busiest people in the world. Ned Bulmer is abroad and busy also, as much so as he can be, his arm in a sling. He is anxious about certain oysters ordered from the city, and is pacified by the response from the gentlemanly body servant,—"The oysters have *arrive*, Mr. Edward, in good order." Boxes are to be unpacked, in which I help. Miss Janet is feverish about the fate of several barrels of crockery. I assist in relieving her. The Major needs my help in opening and unfolding certain cases of fire-works, and in preparing sockets for rockets, and reels for wheels, posts, and platforms, &c., for a display by night. Our Baron, like other Princes, is fond of, and famous for, his pyrotechny. He has invented a new torpedo, by the way, for blowing up the fleet of the Federal Government, whenever they shall attempt to bombard the city; and one of the problems which now occupies his mind, is the preparation of a balloon for dropping hollow shot into the forts of the harbour. The Major is a fierce secessionist. At one time, he rather inclined to co-operation; and I fancy he voted the co-operation ticket for the Southern Congress; but, since the resolutions of the Committee at Columbia, he denounces them as mere simulacra,—using the vernacular for the learned word,—plainly saying, in brief, burly phrase, "Humbugs!"—and has very devoutly sent them all to the devil.

> From Cheves and Chesnut, Burt, Barnwell and Orr,
> To Preston and Pressley, and twenty-five more,
> With Petigru thrown in to make up the score!

But we must eschew politics, in a Christmas Legend, lest we take away some poor devil's appetite for dinner. Our cue is to be genial and gentle, tender and tolerant, not strategetical and tragical.

The fire-works arranged and disposed of, we turned in upon a Christmas Tree, which was to be elevated within the great hall. This was a beautiful cedar, carefully selected, and brought in from the woods, the roots well fitted into the half of a huge barrel, rammed with moss, the base being so draped with green cloth as to conceal the rudeness of the fixture. This, planted and adjusted in its place, we enclosed the piazza, front and rear, with canvas, and hung the interior in both regions with little glass lamps of different colours. Half of the day, Christmas eve, was employed in these and a score of other performances. Nothing that we could think of was omitted. Then, there were boxes of toys for the children to be unpacked, and trunks of pretty presents to be examined, and the names written on them of the persons for whom they were designed. They were, that night, after the guests had all retired, to be suspended to the branches of the Christmas Tree, which was, in the meanwhile, to be kept from sight by the dropping of a curtain across the hall! Ned Bulmer had his gifts prepared, as well as his father and aunt. I, too, had bought my petty contributions, calculating on the persons I should meet.

Before noon, the company began to pour in. Several came to dinner that day. Afternoon brought sundry more, who were to spend the night, and perhaps several nights. The mansion house was entirely surrendered to the ladies and married people;—the young men were entirely dispossessed and driven to sheds and outhouses, in which, fortunately, 'the Barony' was not deficient. Ned and myself lodged with the overseer, and had a snug apartment to ourselves. At dinner, it was already necessary to spread two tables. Every body was becomingly amiable. Care was kicked under the table, and lay crouching there, silent and trembling, like a beaten hound, not daring to crunch even his own bones aloud. The ladies smiled graciously to our sentiments, and we had funny songs and stories when they had gone. After dinner, some of the guests rode or rambled for an hour, others retired to the library,— chess and backgammon; others to the chambers;—and the work of preparation still went on. The holly and the cedar, twined together with bunches of the 'Druid Mistleto,' wreathed the doors and windows, the fire-place, the pictures. Red and blue berries glimmered prettily among the green leaves. At night, we had the tea served sooner than usual, for the Major was impatient for the fire-works. The discharge of a cannon was the signal for crowding to the front piazza. There, as far as the eye could extend, ranging along the green avenue, at equal distances, were piles of flaming lightwood, showing the way to the dwelling. They failed to show the spectators where the Major was preparing for his rockets. Suddenly, these shot up amid the darkness; a flight of a dozen, with the rush of the seraphim, flying, as it were, from the glooms and sorrows of the earth. Then came wheels, Roman candles, frogs, serpents, and transparencies—quite a display, and doing great credit to the Major, besides singing his cheek and hair, and drawing an ounce of blood from his left nostril— the result of a premature and most indiscreet explosion of a turbillon, or something of the sort. But this small annoyance was rather agreeable than otherwise, as tending somewhat to dignify the exploit.

The display over, and the spectators somewhat cooled by standing in the open air, we returned to the rooms and the violin began to infuse its own spirit into the heels of the company. Then followed the dances; quadrilles, cotillon, country dances, Virginny reels, and regular shake-downs. We occupied two saloons at this business till 12 o'clock, when the boys and girls, obeying the signal of Miss Janet, descended to the rooms assigned to offices purely domestic. Huge bowls might here be seen displayed, and mammoth dishes. A great basket of eggs was lifted in sight, and upon a table. Knives and forks, sticks and goose feathers, were put in requisition. Eggs were poised aloft and adroitly cut in twain; the yolk falling into the bowl, the white into the dish— seperating each, as it were, with a becoming sense of what was expected of it. Then the clatter that followed,—the rubbing and the rounding,—the twitching and the clashing! How fair arms flashed, even to the elbow, and strong arms wearied, even to the shoulder blade, to the merriment and mockery of the damsels. With some, the unskilful, *it wouldn't come ;*—in Western par-

lance, ' *they couldn't come it* ';—and the dish had to be transferred
to more scientific hands.   At length, the huge tray being uplifted,
turned upside down, and the white mass clinging still solidly to the
China, it was pronounced the proper moment for reuniting the
parties so recently seperated.   Then rose the golden liquid, a
frosted sea of strength and sweetness and serenity, that never
whispered a syllable of the subtlety that lurked, hidden in the
compound, born of the glowing embraces of lordly Jamaica and
gallant Cognac.   Lo! now the strong-armed youth, as they bear
the glorious beverage on silver salvers to the favourite ladies. They
quaff, they sip, they smile, they laugh; the brightness gathers in
their eyes; they sparkle; the orbs dance like young stars on a
frosty night, as if to warm themselves ;—when suddenly, Miss
Janet rises, stands for a moment silent, looks significantly around
her, and is understood! A gay buzz follows; and, with smiles
and bows, and merry laughter, and pleasant promises, the gay
group disappears, leaving the tougher gender to finish the discussion of that bright, potent beverage, in which the innocent egg is
made to apologize for a more fiery spirit than ever entered into the
imagination of pullet to conceive! Merry were the clamours that
followed;—gay songs were sung;—some of the youngsters, just
from college, took the floor in a stag dance;—while half a dozen
more sallied forth at one o'clock, called up the dogs, mounted their
steeds, and dashed through the woods on a fox hunt.   But the fox
they hunted that night was one of that sort which Sampson let
loose among the Philistines—a burning brand under his brush—
not suffering him to know where he ran!

CHAPTER XVII.

CHRISTMAS—HOW GOLDEN.

CHRISTMAS DAWN! The day opened with bursting of bombs from the laboratory of Major Bulmer. He was up and at work, bright and early, having summoned me to his assistance. In fact neither of us had done much sleeping that night. We had employed more than an hour of the interval, after the termination of the dance, in arranging the gifts among the branches of the cedar, and in other matters. Then we had adjourned to an out-house, where the Major kept his fire-works, and had gotten the explosive pieces in readiness. They did famous execution when discharged, routing every body out of his sleep, though it should be as sound as that of the Famous Seven! The children were all alive in an instant.

"Had old Father Chrystmasse really come."

There was a rush to the chimney places in every quarter, where, the night before, the stockings and satchels had been suspended from the cedar branches. Dear aunt Janet had taken good care that the "Old Father" should make his appearance; and there was a general shout, as each took down his well-stuffed stocking. Ah! how easy to make children happy—how unexacting the little urchins—how moderate in their desires—how innocent their expectations—how pure, if fervent, their little hopes! Treat them lovingly—give them gifts such as love may wisely give—and you impress the plastic and hospitable nature with a true moral for the seventy years of vicissitude that may follow! Ah! shouts of blessed children! as if there lay a sweet bird in the soul, all wing and voice, soaring together in sweetness, earth not yet having stained the one, or made discord in the accents of the other! The dear little creatures! on what sly steps they stole to the several chambers, lingering at the door, waiting to 'catch' the parties as

they issued forth. How they crouched at the entrances of hall
and library; in the porches, behind the doors, beneath the stairs,
under the eaves—wherever their little bodies could find snug har-
bourage—till they could spring out upon the victim. Three of them,
at the same moment, had aunt Janet about the neck. They pulled
off her curls,—they disordered her lace,—they deranged her
handkerchief,—almost entirely demolished her toilet,—and pulled
her down upon the carpet, with their wild-colt displays of affection; and the dear old maid took it all so sweetly, and smiled
through it all, and only begged where she might have scolded, and
promised good things to escape, when she might have threatened
birch and brimstone! And the fierce old Baron, the Major himself, even he, Turk as he is in some respects, he, too, was as
meek under the infliction as if he shared fully the spirit of his sister. The boys and girls, half a dozen in number, seized upon him
as he entered the hall from the court. The girls tugged at arms
and skirts, the boys had him by the neck, arms and shoulders, at
the same moment.

"Merry Christmas, Major";—"Merry Christmas, uncle;"—
"Merry Christmas, grandpa." Merry Christmas saluted him, under all sorts of affectionate titles, from their wild, gay, innocent little
voices. And how graciously the old Sultan submitted to be tugged at
and hugged. How he laughed and tossed them up, and suffered them
to sway him to and fro, until they all came down upon the carpet
in a heap together! There was no growling, or grunting, or com-
plaining; no rebukes and wry faces; but, giving himself up to the
humour of the children, he became for the moment a child himself. And measurably he was. He had kept his heart young,
and could thus still identify himself with the child humours of the
little throng about him. He knew what he had to expect, and had
prepared for them. His pockets were a sort of fairy wallet, such
as we read of in the Oriental and German fables, which is always
giving forth, yet always full. Balls, knives, thimbles, dolls in
boxes, pretty books with gold edges and gay pictures, very soon

unfolded themselves from his several pockets, and each of the happy children took what he pleased. They went off laden with treasures, and making the house ring with cries of exultation.

At sunrise that morning, the egg-noggin passed from chamber to chamber. Why eggs at Christmas as well as Easter? There is a significance in their use, at these periods, which we leave to the theological antiquarian. They are doubtless typical. Enough that, in the Bulmer Barony, the old custom was religiously kept up. Every guest was required to taste, at all events. The ladies mostly, the dear, delicate young things in particular, were each content with a wine-glass. Some of the matrons could relish a full cup or tumbler, and there were some of these who would occasionally find their way into the contents of a second, and—without getting in their cups! We are to graduate the beverage, be it remembered, according to the capacity of the individual; and he alone is the intemperate—we may add the fool also—who takes a power into the citadel which he cannot keep in due subjection.

The bell rings for breakfast. The hour is late. All are assembled. There is joy in all eyes; merriment in all voices; what a singular conventionalism, established by habits so prolonged, for so many hundred years, by which, whatever the secret care, it is overmastered on this occasion, and the sufferer asserts his freedom for a brief day in the progress of the oppressive time! Breakfast at the 'Barony', is, of course, a breakfast for a Prince. Take that for granted, gentle reader, and spare us the necessity to describe. The event over, we group together and disperse. The horses are saddled below. The young gallant lifts his fair one to the saddle. The carriages are ready; and there are parties preparing for a drive. Some of the young men have gone to the woods, pistol and rifle shooting. Others are in the library, companioned by the other sex, at chess and backgammon. We are among these, Ned Bulmer and myself. We have duties at home. We know not what moment will bring to the door our respective favourites. And

13

so, variously engaged and employed, all more or less gratefully, the hours pass until meridian. A little after, the rolling of wheels is heard below. We are at once at the entrance. Major Bulmer is already there. The carriage brings Mrs. Mazyck and her fair daughter. The old lady is not exactly thawed, but the ice is of a thin crust only. The Major tenders her his arm ; mine is at the service of Beatrice. Scarcely have we ascended when other vehicles are heard below. It is now Ned's turn, and while the Major is bowing and supporting Madame Agnes-Theresa, Ned brings in the dear little witch, Paula, hanging on his sound limb, and turning an inquiring and tender glance of interest upon that which pleads for pity from the sling. The Major and his sister divide themselves between the matrons ; while Ned and myself share the damsels between us. We slip out, unobserved, for a walk, leaving the ancient quartette in full chase of parish antiquities, recalling old times and making the passing as pleasant by reflection as possible. Shall I tell you how we strayed, whither we went, what we said together? Not a word of it. If you have heart, you may conceive for yourself; if fancy only, you may trust to conjecture. What is said by young persons, with hearts in full agreement, will seldom bear reporting. It is so singularly the faculty of the heart, under such circumstances, to endow the simplest matters with a rare significance, that ordinary reason becomes utterly unnecessary, and the affections find a speech and a philosophy of far more value, more grateful to the ear, and more profound to the sense, than any that belongs to simple intellect. We were gone fully two hours from the house, yet, so well had the Major and aunt Janet done their parts, we had not been missed by mamma and grandmamma, and neither frowns nor reproaches waited our return. It was evidently fast proving itself a Golden Christmas. The golden period had come round again as so long promised. The lion and the lamb were about to lie down together. That is,—Major Bulmer, seated in the centre of the sofa, with Madame Agnes-Theresa on one hand, and Mrs. Mazyck on the other, had them both in hand as a dextrous driver two fiery and intractable steeds, whom he has subdued; and the free smile playing upon all three countenances, as we entered, was conclusive of such a conjunction of the planets, as held forth the happiest auguries for the future, in respect to the " currents of true love !"

Company continued to arrive. The groups which had ridden forth returned. The house was thronged. The respectable body-servant looked in at the library. The Major rose, went to the door, looked at his watch, came back, said a few words, by way of apology, to the ladies with whom he had been doing the amiable, and then disappeared. The dinner hour was approaching. It was soon signalled. The Major returned. His arm was tendered to Mrs. Mazyck; Madame Agnes-Theresa was served with that of another ancient Major, quite as conspicuous in the parish as he of Bulmer; and then, each to his mates, we followed all in long procession. Need I say, that, while Ned Bulmer, by singular good fortune, was enabled to escort Paula, by the merest accident, I happened to be nigh enough at the moment to yield my arm to Beatrice. Really, the thing was thoroughly providential in both cases.

Such a dinner ! The parish, famous for its dinners, had never seen one like it. It is beyond description. Two enormous tables, occupying the whole length of the spacious dining room, were loaded with every possible form and variety of edible. But the turkey was not allowed, as is usually the case in our country, to usurp the place of honour on this occasion. There was a couple of these birds to each table ; but they stood not before the master of the feast. At our entrance, the space on the cloth was vacant at his end of the table. He stood erect, knife in hand, evidently in expectation. He had one of his famous old English cards to play. One of the turkies was at one of the tables where I was required to preside, the fair Beatrice on my right. The others were interspersed along the two boards. Presently, we heard solemn music without. Then the door was reopened, and the steward, napkin under chin, made his appearance with an enormous dish.

"My friends," quoth the Major, in a speech that was evidently
prepared, and which we abridge to our dimensions, "I am about
to restore a custom common in all the good old English establish-
ments, even within the last hundred years. The turkey has been
raised to quite unmerited honour among us. I am willing to as-
sign him his place upon our table; but I shall depose him from
the first place hereafter. That properly belongs to the Boar's
Head! The Boar's Head was *the* famous dish at Christmas, in
old England; not the turkey. The turkey is an innovation. He
is purely an American fowl, and was utterly unknown in Europe
until after the Spaniards found this continent. He is a respectable bird, particularly in size; but in flavour, cannot rank with the
duck, or even a well-dressed young goose. There is no reason
why he should supersede the Boar's Head. I am willing to give
him the first place on New Year's day, as representing a new era
and a new country; but on Christmas, as a good Christian, I am
bound to stick to the text of the Fathers. Their creed I give you
in their own language, as it was chaunted five hundred years ago.
The steward who placed the Boar's Head on the table, brought it
in with the sound of music, and chaunted, as he advanced, the
following Christmas carol, which, by the way, I have, with the assistance of my young friend, Richard Cooper here, somewhat ventured to modernize to correspond with the vernacular."

The Major then proceeded to repeat, in the formal, sonorous
manner of a schoolboy, whose voice is in the transition state, a
cross between squeak and croak, the following ditty:

> Caput apri defero,
> Reddens laudes Domino!
> "Lo! the Boar's Head, he that spoil'd
> The goodly vines where many toil'd,—
> Merrily masters, be assoil'd,—
> I pray you all sing merrily,
> *Qui estis in convivio.*
>
> The boar's head, you must understand,
> Is the chief service in this land—

And here it lies at your command,
　　Clad in bay and rosemary ;—
　　Servite cum cantico.

With song we bring the wild boar's head,
He spoiled our vines—with mustard spread,
The beast is good and gentle dead,
　　Pray, masters, eat him heartily,—
　　Reddens laudes Domino."

But the Major was not allowed to finish his recitation. We had prepared a surprise for the strategist. Ned and myself, having copies of the carol, had secretly adapted it to appropriate music, and, suffering the Major only to make a fair entrance upon the verse, we broke in with a loud chorus. At first, he stopped and looked at us with a face of doubt. Was it an offence to be resented? We had taken the words out of his mouth. We had converted the recitation into a chant, the chant into a song. Ought he to be angry? A moment decided the question. Certainly, a carol ought to be sung. We had only carried out his purpose more effectually than he was able to do it himself. We had surprised him, but it was a tribute to his objects and tastes that we had prepared in this surprise. The cloud disappeared; he laughed; he clapt his hands; he joined with stentorian lungs in the chorus, and other voices chimed in. We obtained a magnificent triumph.

Meanwhile, the Boar's Head, with a mammoth lemon in his huge jaws, and enveloped in bay leaves and rosemary, was set down in state before us. It was the head of one of the largest of the wild boars that we had slain in our hunt. It was well dressed— it was delicious. Our old English fathers knew what was good ; but I am not sure that any of the ladies partook of the savage dish. "Milk for babes, *meat* for men!" muttered the Major, in a tone between scorn and pity. The feast proceeded, the Baron expatiating occasionally on Boar Heads and Boar Hunts, insisting that, as on every large plantation in the swamp country, wild hogs

13*

were numerous, the proper taste required that we should always have the dish for Christmas. I shall not report his several speeches on this and incidental topics. The champagne made its own frequent reports about this time, and left it rather difficult to follow any orator. The Major now drank with Madame Agnes-Theresa; then with the widow Mazyck, and almost made the circuit of the table, in doing grace with the matrons. The younger part of the company were not slow to follow the example. What sweet and significant things were whispered to the several parties beside us— over the wine, but under the rose. The meats disappeared, the comfits took their place, and disappeared in turn. The best of pleasures find their finale at last. Up rose the ladies, and, with a bumper, well drained in their honour, we followed them to the parlour and the library. A brief pause, and a new summons brought us into the hall. The curtain was raised ; the Christmas Tree was there in all its glory. The doors being closed and the dusk prevailing, the little coloured glass lamps had been lighted among the branches ; and, behind the tree, peering over it, raised upon a scaffolding, stood a gigantic figure—a venerable man, fit to be emblematic of the ancient Jupiter, with a fair, full face, large, mild blue eyes, features bold and expressive, yet gentle ; but, instead of hair, his head was covered with flowing gray moss, and, from his chin, streaming down upon his breast, the gray moss fell in voluminous breadth and burden. He realized the picture of the British Druid. In one hand he bore a branch of the mistletoe, in the other a long black wand, with a silver crook at the extremity. The children clapped their hands as soon as they saw the figure, and cried out,—" Oh ! look at Father Christmas ! Father Christmas ! Father Christmas !" And they were right. Our saint is an English, not a Dutch saint, be it remembered ; and Father Christmas, or the " Lord of Chrystmasse," as he used to be styled, is a much more respectable person, in our imagination, than the dapper little Manhattan goblin whom they call Santa Claus.

With the clamours of the children, the good father was fully awakened to deeds of benevolence. His crook was in instant exercise. The crook with a gift hanging to it, was immediately stretched out to one after the other—a sweet female voice from the back-ground, naming the little favourite as he or she was required to come forward. When the juveniles were all endowed, they disappeared, to weigh and value their possessions; and the interest began for the more mature. The former voice was silent, and that of a man was heard. He named a lady, then another, and another; and as each was called and presented herself at the foot of the tree, the ancient Druid extended his crook towards her, bearing upon it a box, a bag, or bundle, carefully enveloping the gift, her name being written upon it. Soon the voices from the back ground alternated. Now it was a male, now a female voice, each calling for one or other of the opposite sex, until all the tokens of love and friendship were distributed.

"See," said Beatrice Mazyck to me,—"see what the Father has bestowed upon me"; and she showed me a lovely pair of bracelets and a breast pin, in uniform style. She did not see, until I showed her, a plain gold ring at the bottom of the box. She looked at it dubiously, and at me dubiously, tried it on every finger but *the one*, then put it quietly back in the case, and had no more to say on the subject.

But who played the venerable Father, and who played the sweet voices! What matter? Better that the juveniles should suppose that there is an unfamiliar Being, always walking beside them, in whose hands are fairy gifts and favours, as well as birch and bitterness!

CHAPTER XVIII.

DENOUEMENT.

OLD Father Chrystmasse, in the South, does not confine his favours to the palace. The wigwam and the cabin, get a fair portion of his smiles. In other countries, poverty is allowed but a single privilege—that of labour. The right of one's neighbour to work, is that which no one questions any where. In all countries but those in which slavery exists, poverty is supposed to enjoy no other. But there is little or no poverty in the South. Even the slave is rich. He is rich in certainty—security ;—he is insured against cold and hunger,—the two terrible powers, that, more than all others, affright the civilized world. Secure from and against these, the slave is absolutely free from care. He has to work, that is true, but work adapted to one's capacity, suited to one's nature, and not too heavy for one's strength, is perhaps the greatest of all human blessings, since it is the best security for good health and good morals. Cuffee and Sambo are thus secure and thus made happy. But Cuffee and Sambo, like other handsomer and happy people, would never be content with these ; and the good-natured, benevolent, and accommodating Father Chrystmasse has a tree bearing good fruits also for them. When, accordingly, the guests of Major Bulmer had each received his little token of Christian sympathy and good will, the Christmas cedar was removed to the overseer's house, and that night the old Druid officiated behind its branches for the benefit of the negroes. How they crowded and scrambled about, one over the shoulders of the other, each in his best garments, for the favours of the kindly wizard ! There were, among the guests at "The Barony," a learned professor from one of the Northern Colleges, and a young English gentleman, the younger son of a noble house. They watched the scene with a staring curiosity. It enabled them quietly to revise a hundred erring notions and stupid prejudices. When they beheld ten or a dozen superannuated negroes, from whose feeble and failing limbs, sometimes utterly palsied, no labour could be obtained, and who were yet to be fed, and clad, and nursed, and physicked, until Death should close the scene,—negroes who had been in this situation for perhaps a dozen years;—when they beheld fifty more little urchins, barely able to toddle about and be mischievous, who must be provided also with food, clothing and shelter, for which they could give no equivalent in labour for ten or a dozen years at least;—they began to conceive something of that inevitable charity which characterizes the institution of Southern slavery. And when they saw that this charity did not confine itself to the mere necessaries of life, but bestowed its little precious luxuries also;—leaving no pang to poverty,—leaving no poverty;—the slave permitted play and pleasure, and showing at every bound and every breath, and every look and every word, that he lived in his impulses as well as in his limbs,—was permitted to gratify impulses and yearnings, and desires, which the poverty in other lands is only permitted to dream of;—they began to shift and change the argument, and gravely to contend that this was another objection to the institution; that it left the negro in a condition of too much content: in other words, the condition was so agreeable as to leave him satisfied with it. But we will not discuss the matter with such bullet-headed boobies. Enough that Sambo, and Cuffee, and Sibby and Dinah, Tom and Toney, are all making off with something under the arm, derived from the bounty of the benevolent Father Chrystmasse, whom they half believe to be a real personage—a sort of half Deity, half mortal, coming once a year, to see that they are and deserve to be happy. Leaving them in groups about the grounds, we prepare for another display of fire-works, after which we adjourn to the mansion, obedient to the call of the violin.

Supposing you, dearly beloved reader of either gender, the tender and the tough, to be in some degree familiar with the laws of art, you will see that we have this night left only for our *denouément*. The artist is a creator, and so—a Fate. He has established his premises, and the results are inevitable; they bind him just as rigidly as they do his Dramatis Personæ. What we do, accordingly, must be done quickly. The "Golden Christmas" ends with this night, and our parties must be disposed of. Who must be disposed of? How must they be disposed of? Who are the victims? What the processes? You, perhaps, can all of you answer these questions—all except the last. And that is a question to which I can only help you to an answer, as I proceed, and in the natural progress of events. You must not be surprised at this. The artist does not make events; they make themselves. They belong to the characterization. The author makes the character. If this be made to act consistently,—and this is the great necessity in all works of fiction,—events flow from its action necessarily, and one naturally evolves another, till the whole action is complete. Here is the whole secret of the novelist. Now, all that I can tell you of a certainty is this,—that the action must be complete to-night; and that the persons of the story may be expected to exhibit just the same sort of conduct which they have shown from the beginning. More I cannot report. You must judge for yourselves of what you have to expect. You may ask, Shall the sequel be a happy one? That, of course, or it would not be the "Golden Christmas." Will Ned Bulmer be allowed to marry pretty Paula Bonneau? Do you suppose, with such characters as they have shown, they will be happy together? And what of Dick Cooper and Beatrice Mazyck? The question naturally occurs, in answer to this,—What will Tabitha say to it, the housekeeper of that bachelor? But, really, if you thus go on making these inquiries, we shall never make an end of it. Even now, Messrs. Walker, Richards & Co., are crying aloud for "copy," through the lungs of forty printing office fiends. The readers, they cry, are becoming impatient. Nothing, but a marriage, or some other catastrophe, of equal magnitude, will satisfy them. If so—*revenons à nous mouttons!* Let us see what our folks are about.

The tea service over, the fire-works displayed, all preliminaries at an end, the violins in full tune, the dancers are preparing for their partners. Ned Bulmer, arm in sling, is standing in the floor. The Major approaches him with a whisper. His eyes turn upon Beatrice Mazyck.

"Ned, my boy, let me repeat my wishes once more. It is not too late. Paula Bonneau is no doubt a good girl, a fine girl, a pretty girl, but there is no such woman in the parish as Beatrice."

"Father," answered Ned very solemnly, though in a whisper also,—"Your taking the reins out of my hand has already broken my arm: your further attempts at driving me may break my heart."

"Break the d—l!" burst out from the old man, who turned away in a huff. He came up to me, muttering,—

"He's as stubborn as Ben Fisher's mule, that always reared going up hill, and took the studs going down! How to excuse myself to Mrs. Mazyck!"

I could give him neither advice nor consolation; and he wheeled out of the room as soon as he saw that Ned, lame as he was, was taking Paula Bonneau out for the cotillion. I took out Beatrice at the same time. How we danced, with what glee, what perfect abandonment to the influences of the season, must be left to conjecture. Description is impossible. The happiness was not confined to the dances. The elderly folks had their own and various modes of recreation. Some, of course, looked on, enjoying the dancing, just as much as if they themselves had a foot in it. Others were gathered together in side rooms, in the wings, finding solace in conversation; others, apart also, were engaged in whist; and in the hall, or grand passage way, the curtain still being suspended across it, others were preparing for *tableaux*. For these, the characters and scenes were numerous; and a couple of cotillions and a reel being ended, the little bell summoned the spectators to the hall, where, in the area outside of the curtain, they awaited its rising. I was among the actors, and can say nothing of the exhibition, except that it was apparently quite successful with the audience. But it led to other scenes, more important to the event, to which I must hasten. It happened that, among the arrangements, I was cast for the part of Ferdinand, and Beatrice for Miranda, the scene taken from "The Tempest." Beatrice looked admirably the Miranda. Her fair complexion, calm, innocent features, the simple dignity in her expression, the artless grace of her action, all became the presentment wonderfully well. I flatter myself I made a comely Ferdinand enough. I have never doubted that. I am a tolerably good looking fellow, as the world goes. Well—we were together in the library, which we had converted into a sort of green room. We were preparing for the moment when we should be called to the stage. Beatrice had just joined me from the ladies 'tiring room in the rear, and, under the pretence of surveying her costume, I took her hand, held her a little off, and allowed my eyes to devour greedily all her beautiful proportions. There was nobody at that moment in the room. The hall was again empty, the audience having returned to the parlour until the bell should again give the signal when the stage should be occupied. There is a moment in the career of a lover, when some instinct emotion spurs him to an audacity, from which, at most other moments, he would be very apt to shrink. The courage of love wonderfully comes and goes. I was now carried away by mine. The blood rushed in a torrent about my heart. It mounted to my brain, as billows of the sea to the shore. I whispered passionate words ;—I breathed passionate assurances ;—I uttered vows and entreaties in the same breath ; and the bosom of Beatrice heaved beneath her bodice ; and her eyes rose, large and dewy, till they met the gaze of mine. She did not speak, but silently lifted the hand which I clasped, and I beheld the ring which she had found in the Christmas box, securely circling *the* particular finger. Then she spoke, in a tremulous whisper,—

" Was it not your's ?"

I carried the hand to my lips ; the next moment my arm en-

circled her waist; I drew her up to my bosom, and our lips met in
the first most precious kiss of love!

We forgot the world—heard nothing—saw nothing—feared
nothing—in that delicious moment of certain bliss. Little did we
dream, then, that any eye was upon us but that of Heaven. Yet
so it was! It so happened, that the excellent Madame Agnes-
Theresa, looking out for Paula, who had temporarily disappeared,
came to the inner door of the library from the 'tiring room. Her
light footstep was unheard upon the heavy and yielding carpeting.
Our backs were to the door. She beheld us in that first, fond, all-
forgetting embrace—my hand about the waist of Beatrice—her
lips held fast beneath the pressure of mine. Madame Agnes-
Theresa stole away as silently as she came. She was all in a
pleasurable glow of excitement. She had a spice of mischievous
malice in her composition, spite of her Christian benevolence, and
she amiably resolved to make somebody uncomfortable. For me,
she had the best of feelings,—nay, sympathies,—and it really re-
joiced her to see that I was successful with Beatrice. But for Mrs.
Mazyck she had other feelings, equivocal at least, if not unfriendly.
That good lady had a pride equal to her own, and when two proud
planets encounter in the same sky, there is no telling which is most
anxious to put out the light of the other. She suspected the understanding between Major Bulmer and Mrs. Mazyck, for the union
of their two houses, and it did not greatly displease her to see
the scheme defeated. Such being her temper on the subject, she
hurried back to one of the side rooms, where Mrs. Mazyck was
engaged in chat with a little circle; but, on her way, fortunately
for us, encountered our maiden aunt, good Miss Janet Bulmer.
With a chuckle, she whispered in her ears the discovery which she
had made, and hurried onwards. Miss Bulmer immediately conjectured the use which she would make of the secret. With a
more amiable spirit, she immediately hastened to us, and found us
upon the sofa, in an attitude not less significant than that in which

14

Madame Agnes had beheld us. We started up at her en
trance.

"What are you children about?" she asked. "You have been
seen by Mrs. Girardin, and she is so full of the merits of her discovery, that she will surely summon all the world to see it. Here—
to the stage—get out of the way, if you would avoid all sorts of
scandal."

With these words, she hurried us through the private door, and
upon the stage, she herself going out of the large door into the
part of the hall in front of the curtain, and making her way to
the parlour. We closed the door behind us. I then left Beatrice
upon the stage, and throwing a cloak over my gay costume, I
lifted a corner of the curtain, and made for the parlour also. Our
escape was complete, and not made three minutes too soon. The
amiable Madame Agnes, in the mean time, had found Mrs. Mazyck. She was so eager of speech, that she momentarily forgot
her dignity. She stooped over the table, and whispered in the
ear of the latter,—

"Come, quickly, if you would see a couple practising in a tableau which they will hardly show us upon the stage."

Mrs. Mazyck was not unwilling to see sights. She never dreamed,
however, that the desire of her friend was to show her "the Ele-
phant." She got up quickly, and hurried off with her conductor.
Well!—was she gratified? See how events shape themselves
upon one another. It so happened, that, scarcely had we disappeared from the library, than Paula Bonneau entered it, costumed
for Juliet. She was joined the next moment by Ned Bulmer, in
the character of Romeo, his broken arm being concealed by the
dark cloak, with which he only in part disguised his rich attire.
Their love experience was not so recent and fresh as that of Beatrice and myself. They had no preliminaries to overcome.

"Why, Paula, my nonpareil, you look a thousand times love-
lier than ever." And he caught her in his arms, and she lifted
her little mouth, as if she quite well knew what was coming, and—

Mrs. Mazyck stood at the door, with Madame Agnes-Theresa, utterly confounded, looking over her shoulder! She had come to witness a very different scene, or with very different parties. She was dumb—done up—dead—all in an instant. That one glance show-ed her all the world in confusion. She began to listen for the thunder. She took for granted that a world's hurricane, wrecking every thing, was about to break loose. In the twinkling of an eye, she thought of all the conflagrations and disasters that had ever threatened and devoured mankind. She thought of the French Revolution; the explosion of Mount Vesuvius; the massacre of the Holy Innocents ; the crusades and death of Saint Louis ; the great fire in Charleston, which destroyed St. Philip's Church ; the late snow storm which had demolished her orange trees ; the burning of the Richmond theatre; the killing of the hundred school-children in New York, and the speeches of Kossuth and Lola Montes. All these terrible things and thoughts rushed through her brain in the same moment ;—all together, piled up one on top of the other,— rolled together, one in the wrappings of the other—Mount Vesu-vius head over ears in the snow storm, and Kossuth and Lola Montes, somehow busy with the guillotine and the Parisi-ans, in the Reign of Terror. The poor old lady had prepared a terrible surprise for herself, and was ' hoist with her own petard.' " One stupid moment motionless she stood," and, all the while, the lips of Romeo were doing fearful execution, spite of her struggles, upon those of the lovely little Juliet.

You should have seen the quiet, sly, expressive glance of Mrs. Mazyck, looking round and upward into the vacant visage of her companion. It said volumes. It did not need that she should whisper—" truly, this is a tableau, such as they never would have given to the public !" That glance restored our venerable grand-mother to speech.

The sounds broke forth in a sort of sobbing shriek.

" Why, Paula,—Paula Bonneau, I say !"

Then the guilty couple started, looking fruitlessly round for the means of escape, hardly seeming to conjecture where the sounds came from, and both utterly dumb with consternation. Never was surprise, on all sides, so complete. Says Mrs. Mazyck satirically,—

"Why, Mrs. Girardin, was this, indeed, the tableau which you meant *me* to see."

The good grandmother gave her a savage look, then pushed by her, and striding into the room, confronted the young people.

"Paula Bonneau, can I believe my eyes."

The exigency of the case made the little damsel strong. She lifted her eyes to the face of the old lady: her voice grew strong; her heart recovered all its courage.

"Yes, mamma, it is true, I love Mr. Bulmer, and he loves me, and———"

"Indeed! Do I hear? Can I believe my own ears? Why, Paula Bonneau, this is the most astonishing boldness. I'm ashamed for you! Was ever heard such language!"

"It is plain enough!" quoth Mrs. Mazyck, drily, and she seemed greatly to enjoy the consternation of the grandmother. The latter gave her another fierce look and proceeded.

"Oh! mamma, you must not be angry!" cried the dear little girl, now attempting to throw her arms about the old lady, who resisted the endearment. "It is true, mamma, what I tell you. I love Edward more than any other person. I will never marry any man but Edward."

"Heavens! what a child! You will never marry any other man! What impiety—what indelicacy! And you will force yourself into a family which hates and despises *your* family—which will always look upon you as an intruder—"

Here Ned Bulmer found an opportunity to interfere. His courage returned to him at the right moment.

"No, Mrs. Girardin, never! You do us wrong, madam, very great wrong, I assure you. You and your family—we shall—"

He was arrested in his speech. His father, who had entered the room unseen, now interposed.

"It is proper that I should speak now," said he. "Mrs. Girardin, let me plead with you for these young people. I have not urged or countenanced this proceeding in any way; in fact, I have hitherto opposed it; not because of any objection or dislike to you or your family which, now, I honestly respect and honour, but because I had looked in another quarter for my son. But, since my choice, is not his, I owe it to him, and to your daughter, to do all I can to make them happy. Their young hearts refuse to follow the course which ours would prescribe for them; and, perhaps, they are the wiser, and will be the happier for it. We would have perpetuated prejudice and hatred between our families; they will drive out these evil spirits with Love. Let us not oppose this better influence. Let me entreat you to forego your frowns. Give them your blessing, as here, at this blessed season, when all the influences of life are meant to be auspicious to human happiness, I freely bestow upon them mine. My son has thwarted some of my most favourite wishes; but shall I not make my son happy if I can? Will you be less merciful to your daughter? Take her to your arms, my dear madam, and let our families, hitherto separated by evil influences, be now united by blessing ones."

The voice of Mrs Mazyck sounded immediately in my ears, for by this time I had joined the circle also.

"Mr. Cooper, will you be pleased to order my carriage."

Though her words were addressed to me, they were loud enough to be heard over the whole room. Major Bulmer started and approached her. She turned away at his approach. But he was not a man to be baffled.

"Nay, nay, Mrs. Mazyck," he said gently, taking her hand— "this must not be. You must not be angry with me, my dear madam, because I failed to do what I wished, and had believed myself able to do. I have been disappointed—defeated in my purpose—and I honestly assure you that I greatly regret it.— Though compelled to yield now to an arrangement which seems

14*

inevitable, yet I do so with real sorrow. I should greatly have preferred the arrangement which would have given my son to your daughter—"

Another voice now arrested that of the Major. It was that of Beatrice Mazyck. The explosion in the library had brought her down from the stage where I had left her, as Miranda, and she had been a silent auditor and spectator of the scene, in which she now found it necessary to take part. She touched the Major on his arm, and said, in a whisper—

"I thank you, Major Bulmer, for your good intentions; but mother and yourself were greatly mistaken in this matter. Let me say to you, now, and prevent further mistakes, that the proposed arrangement was quite impossible. Ned Bulmer knew perfectly well, long ago, that we were not made for each other. We have been friends quite too long to suffer any misunderstanding between us on any such subject. So, I beg you to relieve yourself of all further disquiet in regard to it, and if you will suffer me to take mamma into the other room, I will soon satisfy her, that if there be anybody to blame in the business, I am the person. Mamma—"

And she took the arm of the severe lady, but paused for a moment, and said in undertones to me—"Don't order the carriage." The mother heard her.

"But, why not? I am about to go."

"You *can't* go, mamma. I will show you good reasons for it."

And the two went into the 'tiring room together. They were gone full half hour, and when I met them again, they were in the parlour, the mother apparently resigned to her fate. I saw at a moment that the revelation had been made. The maternal eyes rested on me with a searching expression, full of meaning,—not exactly placid, I confess, but not severe. The way was opened for me, and I had to do the rest.

Meanwhile, the progress in the library, with the other parties, had reached a similar conclusion. The feud between the rival houses of Bulmer and Bonneau, was adjusted. An hour later, in the parlour, standing before the fire, John Bull fashion, the Major rubbed and clapped his hands together, with as much glee as if his projects had succeeded just as he had devised them.

"This," said he, "is, indeed, a Golden Christmas. Two pair of hearts made happy to-night. Positively, ladies, I could be tempted to look about me myself, for a consoler in the shape of a wife. I feel quite as young as at forty. I am not ice. There is still a warm current about my heart, that almost persuades me to be in love. Ah! if I could find somebody to smile upon me!"

And he looked, comically fond, now upon Mrs. Mazyck, and now upon Madame Agnes-Theresa. The former lifted a proud head, and the latter waved her fan deliberately between her face and the Major's glances, as if dreading their ardency. The latter was too wary to continue the subject. He changed it rapidly, and, being in a free vein of speech, he gave us a most interesting history of the settlement of "The Barony," by his great grandfather. This involved a full account of the ancient feuds of the Bulmer and Bonneau families, showing how it was begun, and how continued through successive generations. The episode, had we space, should be given here. It was full of animation and adventure, and gave an admirable picture of early life in the colony.— The subject was a favourite one with the Major, and he handled it with equal skill, spirit and discretion. We must reserve it for a future Christmas Chronicle. The reader may look for it some day hereafter, God willing, under the title of "The Ancient Feud between the Houses of Bulmer and Bonneau." They shall form our York and Lancaster histories in time to come. Enough, that we succeeded in healing the feud after royal example—blending our roses, white and red, for the benefit of other hearts that do not know how to be happy—showing them how to throw down the barriers of prejudice, hate, self-esteem and superstition, by letting the heart, under natural impulses, act according to its own nature, and under those benign laws which are privileges rather than laws.

Well!—what need of further delay?—Does it need that I should say we went to supper that night, after all our excitements?—Say what we had for supper, and who ate, and who, with hearts too full already, had no appetite for meaner food? And that the old ladies went finally to bed; that the young ones followed them; that the lads *would* wind up the night with egg-nog, and that some did not go to bed at all? We may dispense with all this.

> " So may the fates,
> The future fashion, that it shall not cheat
> The true fond hearts which welcome it."

EARLY in January, at the entreaties of Major Bulmer himself, Ned led Paula Bonneau to the altar. We had a famous wedding. Are you curious to know how fares that other couple with whose *affairè du cœur* I have somewhat employed your attention? Ask Tabitha, my present housekeeper. Nay, hear her, what she says to me, at the moment I am writing.

" Look yer, Mass Dick, wha' dis, I yer?"

" What, Tabitha?"

" Old Sam Bonneau bin to de gate yesterday, and he say you and Miss Be'trice Mazyck guine to get married in two mont' from now. You no bin tell me nothing 'bout 'em."

" No, Tabitha; but now that you have heard it, I may as well confess the truth. God willing, the thing will happen."

" Spec' den, Mass Dick, you no want me wid you in de housekeeping. Don't 'tink I kin 'gree wid young woman that lub see heap o' people—and keeps much comp'ny, and is always making fuss ob house cleaning, and brushing up, and confusions among sarbants."

" Can't do without you, Tabby. You must try Miss Beatrice. I think you'll get on very well with her."

" Bin git on berry well widout 'em," growled my domestic Hecate as she flung herself out of the breakfast-room.

HERE ends our story. 'Story, quotha!' The reader is half inclined to blaze out at the presumption which dignifies, with the name of story, a narrative which has neither duel, nor robbery, nor murder—neither crime nor criminal. Yet, not too fast. It so happens that there was a criminal that Christmas, and a crime, at the 'Barony.' and I may as well give the affair, as it concerns two of the persons employed in our chronicle. You remember Jehu, the coachman of Miss Bulmer? He was the criminal. The crime committed was theft. The thing stolen was a fine fat shoat, the property of Zacharias, the gentlemanly body servant of Major Bulmer. Zacharias made his complaint the day after Christmas. Jehu was brought up for examination at the home of the overseer. Zack stated his case in the most gentlemanly style and language. He was the owner of seven hogs. The shoat stolen was one of the fattest. He had designed it for his New Year's dinner. He had invited certain friends to dine with him on that day—Messrs. Tom, Tony, Peter, Sam, Fergus, &c.,—gentlemen of colour, belonging to certain planters of the neighbourhood. His shoat disappeared two days before. Jehu gave a supper on Christmas night. On that occasion the stolen shoat was served up to numerous guests.

Here Jehu, shifting his position so as to transfer the weight of his body from his right to his left leg, and throwing his head sideways upon his left shoulder, put in snappishly—

"Ax 'em, maussa, ef he no eat some of de pig he se'f."

The question was accordingly put. Zacharias admitted that, as the guest of Jehu that night, he had partaken of his own pig. He was ignorant of that fact. Had he known it while eating, he does not know what might have been the consequence. He might have been very angry—he might have been taken ill. He would have felt deeply the death of the favourite shoat, cut off before its appointed time.

The case was fully established. But Jehu insisted upon his merits in making a frank and free confession.

"I won't tell you bit o' lie, maussa. You know, maussa, I always bin tell you, I can't help it—I must tief pig. I nebber, so long as I know dis place, bin tief noting else but pig. Maussa, you trus' me wid heep o' tings—Miss Janet, him trus' me wid heep o' tings— clothes, hank'chif, money, silber spoon, ebbry ting—nobody kin say Jehu ebber tief so much as a copper wort'. But maussa, I can't help it—I must tief pig. Fat pig aint mek for run an grunt jis' where he please, and nebber gee anybody brile and sassage. I can't le' 'em pass. I must knock em ober when I see 'em so fat and sassy.— Der's a someting mek me do it, maussa. Der's a somebody dat's a saying in my ear all de time—'kill de pig, Jehu!' I kill 'em: I kill Zach pig—I tell you trute, maussa—da me kill 'em—but wha' den? Ef Zach had a bin say to me—'Jehu, da's a fat pig o' mine—I guine kill 'em and hab supper New Year night, Jehu, and you shall hab taste ob 'em, wid de oder coloured gentlemen sarbants,'—ef he bin say dat to me, maussa, I nebber bin touch he pig. But he nebber say de wud, maussa; ax 'em ef he ebber say sich 'ting to me."

Zacharias admitted that he had been guiltless of the suggested civility; but he submitted whether he was required to do so, un- less he pleased it; and whether his forbearance to do so, afforded any justification to Jehu, for slaughtering his innocent porker be- fore its time. The subject was one of grave discussion, and was closely argued. Jehu particularly insisted upon it, thinking it *a great point gained to establish the allegation. His next point was of like character, and he urged it with even more tenacity.

"Zach," said he, "ent I come to you, cibbil, like a gentleman, and ax you to my supper?"

Zach admitted the civility. But, by the way, he took care to insinuate that he thought his acceptance a great condescension, to which he was influenced simply by the nature of the season— Christmas inculcating condescension among the other charities.— He was by no means an admirer of Jehu—did not rank him among his acquaintance—thought his manners decidedly vulgar—

thought his language particularly low. But was himself of an indulgent and amiable temper, and frequently condescended, through mere charity, to the sacrifice of good taste. He now avowed his resolution never to be caught in such company again.

Jehu eyed him savagely while he made this answer, as a wild western hunter would eye a Broadway dandy, making a similarly complacent speech, with the secret determination to 'take the change out of him,' the moment he caught him on the high road.

"Ax um, ef he no eat hearty ob de pig, maussa."

Zacharias admitted that the pig was well-dressed, in excellent condition, and his own appetite was not amiss. He was not troubled much with indigestion. Had on some occasion suffered from this disease, but not latterly.

The evidence was finished. Jehu was called upon for his defence. He made it with rare audacity. Admitted that he could not resist the temptation to steal hog meat. It was a law of his nature that he should steal it. Denied that he ever felt a disposition to steal anything else. Thinks that if Zacharias had given him due notice of his intention to kill the shoat for New Year's night, and had included him among the invited guests, he might have withstood the Tempter. Admits that the right of property in most things is sacred. Doubts, however, whether there can be any right of property in pigs. Owns pigs himself. Would'nt be hard upon one who should steal *his* pigs; but, added slyly, that, knowing the tempting character of fat pig, he never encouraged his in becoming so. It did not need; there were always a sufficient number of fat pigs about for his purposes. To conclude, Jehu held it to be a justification of his offence, that Zach kept his pig fat and did not kill him—that, when he resolved to kill, he betrayed a niggardly (not *niggerly*—a negro is seldom niggardly, by the way,) unwillingness to give any portion of the supper to him, the said Jehu ; and that, when the pig was stolen snd slaughtered, he was honourable enough to invite the owner to partake of the feast, which was not confined to pig only. There were sundry other excellent dishes—a fowl, a flitch of rusty bacon, a peck of potatoes, and no less than fourteen loaves of corn bread. Jehu boldly threw himself upon the virtue of his case and of the court, and the spirit of justice prevailing in the land.

They did not suffice for his safety. He was found guilty, and sentenced to the loss of three of his *lean* pigs to Zacharias, in compensation for his fat one. The Major said to him, however— "If you keep honest till next New Year's, Jehu, and kill no more fat pigs of other people, I will give you three out of my stock."

The decision did not seem to give that satisfaction to either party, which was anticipated from it. Jehu growled between his teeth unintelligibly, while Zacharias openly suggested his fears that when he had fattened the three hogs thus assigned him, they were still in the same danger of being stolen and eaten in consequence of the reckless voracity of the offender's appetite for hog's flesh, and his loose ideas on the subject of pig property. Says the Major quickly—

"If he eats your pigs again, Zach, you shall eat him."

"Thank you, sir," quoth the gentlemanly Zacharias, with a look of sovereign disgust, "but, don't think, sir, such meat would set easy on my stomach."

There was a laugh, and Ned Bulmer, with that pernicious propensity to punning, which was perpetually popping into play, exclaimed—

"Zach would be evidently better satisfied, before such a meal, that the meat should be well *dressed*." And he shook his twig whip significantly over the shoulders of the criminal. No ways discomfitted, Jehu, with a dogged reiteration of his moral nature, growled out as he retired—

"Lick or kill, jes de same—dis nigger can't help tief fat pig in sassage time."

THE END.

CPSIA information can be obtained
at www.ICGtesting.com
Printed in the USA
LVOW08s0259130117
520681LV00019B/67/P